*I was running for my life. . . .*

It was after me. Right on my tail. I could hear the weird, high whine of its motor, like an evil dentist's drill. It made me run faster.

Up ahead I could see the bombed-out shell of an old building. Crumbling walls, exposed girders. If I made it there, I could maybe find a hiding spot. Something to crawl behind. A way to escape.

I was almost there. Another twenty yards.

I could practically feel its laser sights locking right between my shoulder blades. It made the skin there prickle. My legs strained, my sneakers pounded on the rocky ground—

And then they were pedaling against nothing but air. The ground had disappeared. I pitched forward, thrown off balance, and it was suddenly dark and I was falling, falling. . . .

# mindwarp ™

*Alien Terror*
*Alien Blood*
*Alien Scream*
*Second Sight*
*Shape-shifter*
*Aftershock*
*Flash Forward*

Available from MINSTREL® Paperbacks

# mindwarp ™

# Flash Forward

by

Chris Archer

A MINSTREL® BOOK

Published by POCKET BOOKS

New York   London   Toronto   Sydney   Tokyo   Singapore

# To Johnny

A MINSTREL PAPERBACK *Original*

A Minstrel Book published by
POCKET BOOKS, a division of Simon & Schuster Inc.
1230 Avenue of the Americas, New York, NY 10020

mindwarp™ is a trademark of Daniel Weiss Associates, Inc.
Produced by 17th Street Productions, a division of
Daniel Weiss Associates, Inc., New York

ISBN: 0-671-02167-2

First Minstrel Books printing August 1998

10  9  8  7  6  5  4  3  2  1

A MINSTREL BOOK and colophon are registered trademarks of
Simon & Schuster Inc.

Printed in the U.S.A.

# Chapter 1

# Ashley

My name is Ashley Rose. For all thirteen and three-quarter years of my life, I have lived in the town of Metier, Wisconsin. I even died in it once.

But that's another story.

You've probably heard of Metier. It's been on TV a couple of times. Mostly on those cheezoid shows with titles like *Weird Universe* or *Unexplained Mysteries.* The kind that feature stories on Big Foot and crop circles and alien visitations.

Metier falls into that last category. In fact, over the years we've become pretty famous as a place for UFO sightings. So many people here say they've seen strange lights at night that we've been nicknamed the Roswell of the North.

I never used to believe in the stories. But that was before my thirteenth birthday. Before I found out I wasn't like most kids. Before my life became one mind-warping test of survival after another.

You wouldn't guess it to look at me. On the outside, I look just like an average junior high student. *Too* average, if you ask me. If you saw me on the street or in line at the movies, you wouldn't even look twice—especially if you're a boy.

I have light brown hair and plain brown eyes, which I

get from my father. From my mother I got the silver blood, supersensitive hearing and vision, the ability to stay underwater as long as I want, and the power to regenerate new parts of my body if they get cut off. (Don't ask how I found out about that last one.)

Of course, Mom didn't tell me about my powers. She vanished without a trace when I was four years old.

She didn't tell me about the evil, shape-shifting aliens who would try to hunt me down when I turned thirteen, either. I had to find it all out for myself.

But luckily not *by* myself.

Because there were other kids in Metier whose parents mysteriously disappeared when they were four. Kids who also developed special powers on their thirteenth birthdays—and who also got a visit from the alien hunters.

Two of them—Todd Aldridge and Elena Vargas—didn't escape the aliens that were sent for them.

The others—Ethan Rogers, Jack Raynes, Toni Douglas and me—were luckier.

And until today, our luck had held out.

Two hours ago the aliens had trapped the four of us remaining kids in our town's deserted mall. They weren't taking any chances on our getting away. They cut the power and the phone lines and blocked off all the exits. Then they crashed their UFO right through the skylight over the food court. They must have expected us to put up quite a fight. We did.

What they *hadn't* expected was that we'd hijack their UFO, leaving them behind.

But we did that, too.

It seemed like a good idea at the time.

Unfortunately for us the ship was preprogrammed to return to the aliens' planet. And once aboard, we had no way of turning it back. Amazingly the entire trip only lasted a couple of minutes.

But the biggest surprise didn't come until we exited the UFO. . . .

"I don't believe this," I now whispered in shock. "This can't be real. It *can't* be."

We were standing outside the hatchway of the hijacked alien craft. The silver ship crouched above us on six spindly metal legs, looking like a giant metallic beetle.

Before us, stretching as far as the eye could see, was a hostile, alien-looking wasteland. It looked like the set for a movie about an interplanetary war—and it *wasn't* the planet that had won.

A dry, foul wind whistled over the rubble of ruined buildings. Dust swirled in craters left by massive explosions. Above, the sun was white-hot and strangely intense.

My thoughts were like a tiny scream inside my head. *I want to go home. I want to go home.*

The problem was . . . we already *were* home.

In front of us, half buried in the dirt and sand, was a ten-foot-high letter *M*. At one point it had been part of a sign hanging outside the front entrance of the Metier Mall. Now the mall was just a charred, bombed-out shell.

The large brass letter was all that was left, and it was corroded and tarnished green by the polluted atmosphere.

The UFO wasn't a spaceship. *It was a time machine.*

It hadn't brought us to another planet. It had brought us into the future.

"Anybody want to see if the food court is still open?" Jack cracked. "I could go for a pizza with everything. Make that *double* everything."

"Why don't you hold the jokes for a while, Jack?" Ethan replied. "We've got to think of a plan."

"*Hello?*" said Toni. "Don't you think it's a little *late* for that? Look around you. The earth has been destroyed. It's over. We lost."

I was suddenly struck by a sickening thought. "What if somehow those aliens we left behind caused all this? This could all be our fault!"

"You can't think like that," Ethan said. "First of all, we didn't lose. We escaped. Second of all, we had no choice in the matter. No one knew the ship was a time machine or that it would take us here. But now that we know, we just have to get back."

"And how do you suggest we do that," Jack asked, "by *walking* back to our time? Because I think they only built this buggy to go one way."

It was true. No sooner had we landed than the UFO went dead, like a stalled car. Even Toni's power—the ability to conduct and channel electricity—was no use in powering it back up.

"Maybe there's some kind of an emergency override,"

Ethan suggested, "or maybe we can figure out a way to trick it into turning back on."

"What difference does it make?" I said, waving my arms around helplessly. "If this is Earth's future, it doesn't matter if we make it back to the past. Not when we already know how this movie ends."

"This isn't a movie," Ethan countered, "it's real life. And who knows how time travel works? This is the future, but it might just be a *possible* future. It doesn't *have* to happen. Maybe, if we can figure out what caused all this, we can travel back in time and stop it. Change the course of history."

"Yeah, well, you can talk about changing the future all you want," Jack said. "But in the immediate present, I'm about to pass out from hunger. How are we going to find food? How are we going to find water? I'm guessing the nearest vending machine is about three thousand light-years away."

"I'm sure we'll find some water out there . . . somewhere," Ethan replied, though from his tone, I don't think even he believed himself. He started patting the pockets of his jeans. "As for food, well, I can do something about that."

Reaching into his front pocket, he withdrew what looked like a small red, white, and blue plastic doll. It was some superhero—Captain America, I think. I always knew that Ethan was into comic books, but this was taking things a little too far.

Then Ethan tilted the doll's head back and a small

purple candy popped out of its neck. It was a Pez dispenser.

He held one of the violet candies out to Jack. "It isn't much, but it's better than nothing. At least the sugar will keep us going until we can find real food."

Jack took the candy. "The world's largest collection of Pez dispensers is owned by Zachary Kolodny of Farmingdale, New York," he said mechanically. Jack was always reciting some bit of trivia he'd memorized from *The Guinness Book of World Records.* It could get annoying, especially when he did it in one of the thousands of foreign languages he could speak.

Toni laughed bitterly. "Look around, Jack," she said. "The largest collection of Pez dispensers is right there in Ethan's hand."

That brightened him up some. "Wow," Jack said. "I bet I could set any record I wanted."

"Sure," I told him. "It's not like there's much competition."

"Fattest man, thinnest man," Jack said.

"Worst haircut," Toni suggested.

"Ethan, you've got a lock on oldest," I told him, grinning.

"Alive, anyway," Ethan stated, not returning my smile.

It was a sobering thought. Could everyone on Earth be dead? Were we the only ones left? I shuddered, not wanting to think about what had happened to the people I'd left behind, like my father and my best friend, Jenny Kim. Had they somehow survived? Had *anyone* survived?

Something had happened to turn the earth into this wasteland. *When* it happened was anybody's guess. How

6

far into the future had we come? Two months? Two years? Two *thousand* years? It was time to find out.

"Let's do it," I said. "I'm not beaten. Let's explore a little and try to figure out what happened here. Then see if we can't turn the tables on those bug-eyed creeps."

The others stared at me. I'm not usually the one who takes charge. "I'm with Ashley," Toni said. "Girl power, right?"

"Are you in, Jack?" Ethan asked. "We can't do it without you."

"I suppose," Jack said, sighing heavily. "But I can already tell, it's all going to end in tears."

"Fine," Ethan told him. "Let's just hope they're alien tears."

Moments later we were trudging across the surface of the strange planet. The fact that it was the same one I'd grown up on only made the whole thing stranger.

I hoped that no one saw how badly I was shaking.

# Chapter 2

# Toni

As we headed into the barren terrain I should have said something, but all I could think was, *Isn't there an easier way to do this? Preferably one where I don't have to get dirty?*

Ahead of me, Ashley Rose was shaking like a leaf. I can't say that I blamed her.

We were trudging through the burned-out remains of what had once been my favorite place in the entire world—the Metier Mall. I do not like trudging. I am a delicate and sensitive person, with delicate and sensitive skin. When I am forced to do something like trudge through miles of broken glass and rubble, it makes me want to break someone's nose. Instead I made a mental list of all the vocabulary words I knew that described my surroundings: *decimated, demolished, depopulated, desolate, devastated—*

Ashley suddenly stopped walking. "Do you hear something?" she asked.

"You mean, other than Jack's stomach?" I replied.

Ashley cocked her head, listening intently, like a spaniel. "No . . . more like a low humming noise."

"I don't think there's anything out here," I reassured her. "I don't hear anything, either," Jack offered, "nor do

I see anything. Most importantly, I don't *taste* anything. What I smell is too disgusting to mention, and the only thing I feel is that the sun here seems like it's set on stun. What are we doing out here? Let's go back to the ship."

"I second the motion," I said.

"I don't think we should go back to the ship," Ethan warned. "The thing came here by autopilot. That means the aliens know where to find it. And if they know where to find it, then they'll be coming for it."

"What aliens?" I asked him. "Does this look like a place where anyone would live? I think that this entire planet is uninhabited."

"I hate to agree with Toni, but she's got a point," Jack chimed in. "What if when those aliens tried to stop us from blasting off, they damaged the ship so badly that it took us here by accident?"

"Or what if there was some kind of booby trap that we set off," I added, "like a car alarm for time machines? Unless you turn it off, it takes you here. Go straight to the end of the world, do not pass go, do not collect two hundred dollars."

"Okay, guys, I hear what you're saying," Ethan started, "but I still think—"

Ashley cut him off with a big "shhh!" She had her fingers pressed to her temples and seemed to be straining to listen to something. She looked like she was trying to pick up a radio broadcast—without the radio. "I'm *telling* you," she insisted, "I can hear a humming, and it's getting louder!"

"Ashley," I told her, "look around. Do you see anyone

here?" I gestured at the surrounding rubble. "There's not a single sign of li—"

Then the world exploded in a shower of rocks and fire and I was spinning through the air.

I didn't see what had hit me. Not at first. But the ground beside me was still smoking from the enormous laser-beam blast that had carved out a crater the size of a satellite dish.

I turned over and tried to stand, but I was still dizzy. No sooner had I moved than a second laser blast hit.

The next thing I knew, a strong arm was helping me up—Jack's—and we were running over the uneven terrain. "What was that?" I screamed as we ran. "What's attacking us?"

"Don't look now," Jack told me, "but we're being chased by the world's largest eyeball."

I glanced behind me. What I saw chilled my blood. Our attacker was a metal sphere, about five feet in diameter and gleaming brightly under the harsh sun. It was hovering at least fifteen feet in midair, and it was humming—making a horrible mechanical whine that was steadily building in pitch. As I watched, a metallic "eyelid" opened to reveal a thick layer of glass. At its center, forming the iris, was a glowing red cylinder that I knew instantly was a laser cannon.

The humming reached a fever pitch. A second later a red-hot laser beam sliced into the rubble at our heels, hurling sharp rocks against the back of our legs. When my ears recovered from the blast, I noticed that the humming was much lower. But it quickly began to rise once more.

*It's recharging*, I realized.

Jack must have realized this, too, for his grip on my hand grew tighter as we ran for our lives, Ashley and Ethan close behind us.

"We've got to split up!" Ethan shouted.

"What?" I cried. "How will we find each other?"

"Never mind that," Ethan yelled. "There's only one of it, and there's four of us. If we split up, we've got better odds."

"Yeah—all except for the one it chooses," Jack yelled back.

But we knew Ethan was right. We had no choice. The logical thing to do was to separate; it couldn't follow all of us.

The humming had once again reached the danger level. Just as the newest laser blast tore into the earth we scattered like four fighter pilots breaking formation.

I didn't look back. I knew the eyeball was after me. I could hear it. Adjusting its sights.

I ran.

I zigged and zagged, trying to make myself as much of a moving target as possible. I raced over chunks of broken asphalt and hurdled over the charred, petrified remnants of fallen trees. I fell a couple of times but always picked myself up and kept running.

It wasn't until I'd been running for a good two minutes that I realized the humming had disappeared. The eyeball thing wasn't chasing me, after all.

I slowed down and then stopped. My lungs were burning. My legs felt like rubber bands. I turned around.

There was no sign of the eyeball. I scanned the skies, the horizon. Nothing.

Then I saw a dart of motion in the distance. I saw a figure—Ashley, I think—ducking behind what looked like a low wall.

I dashed over to join her.

The wall actually turned out to be an old steel-and-concrete staircase that was lying on its side. What happened to the building it had been attached to was anybody's guess.

Jack was already there.

"Fancy meeting you here," he said to me as I slid in beside him.

"You call this fancy?" I replied.

"Guys," Ashley warned, her voice trembling with fear, "I think it's gone, but please, keep your voices down."

"Hey, wait a second," Jack said. "If *three* of us are hiding here . . ."

"Then the ball must be chasing Ethan," I said softly.

"And he's all by himself," Jack added.

"Come on," Ashley said, standing up. "We've got to find him."

At first we tried sneaking from hiding place to hiding place, scanning the horizon for any sign of Ethan or the laser-shooting sphere. But both had disappeared without a trace.

Eventually we began walking around in the open—even calling out Ethan's name. But he never shouted back. Nearly

12

two hours later it seemed as if we had covered the entire surrounding area without finding so much as a footprint.

Night was falling. Only a thin sliver of the sun peeked over the horizon, looking like a brilliant red thumbnail. As the sky grew darker the wind picked up. I was quickly turning into a human icicle.

*Great,* I thought, *cold and hungry. What's next—allergies?*

"Look," Jack broke in, "we all want to find Ethan. But if we don't find shelter before dark, we're going to freeze to death. And if we're dead, that'll make it real hard to search for him."

"What do you propose?" Ashley asked sarcastically. "I forgot to pack my tent."

"I think we should head back to the ship," he replied. "It's warm there."

"I agree," I said, a little too quickly.

"Isn't that exactly what Ethan said not to do?" Ashley asked.

"Yeah," Jack replied, "but Ethan didn't realize we'd be out here this long. If he did, he might have changed his mind."

"I don't think we have a choice," I said.

Ashley looked like she wanted to argue further, but she was just too tired. "Fine," she said wearily, "lead the way."

Jack and I looked at each other. "Don't you know where it is?" he asked me.

*Here we go again.* "Don't *I* know where it is?" I asked. "I thought *you'd* know where it was. After all, you're the one who flew it here."

"Can't you use your special ability and, like, make a compass or something?" Jack demanded.

13

"Can't you use your special ability and, like, call its name?" I said back.

"I think we landed over there," Ashley said, cutting us off, "past that rise. Let's go before the two of you actually get into a fistfight."

The good news is, Ashley was right. The landing site *was* beyond the rise. The bad news is, the *ship* wasn't there anymore.

"Okay. W-w-wait a minute. Let's th-think this through," Jack said through chattering teeth. "M-m-maybe this isn't the landing site."

"*Hello?* Do you even *see* this?" I said, walking over to the giant letter *M* that protruded from the ground. "The ship was parked right here, in section *M*. *M* as in Metier Mall. *M* as in missing. *M* as in *moron!*"

"*M* as in *mental,*" Jack retorted. "You n-n-need to chill, Toni."

"*Chill?*" I shouted. "*Th-th-that's* a good one."

I read once that the night in a desert is as cold as the day is hot. What can I say? Our hometown had become the next Sahara.

"We've got to stop fighting," Ashley said, "and figure out where we'll spend the night."

"F-f-fine by me," Jack stuttered.

"If we stack up some of the loose rubble, we can make a breakfront against the wind," Ashley said. "It'll help keep us warm. Then if we dig a pit and huddle close together in it, we should retain enough body heat to make it until morning."

Ashley was always surprising me by how resourceful

she became in crisis situations. I could see that she was scared—who wouldn't be, under the circumstances?—but she wasn't panicking. Just the opposite: She was showing us how to survive.

I looked at Jack. Ashley's last words were sinking in. We'd have to huddle close together until morning. Ugh. Sometimes I think survival is overrated.

"Let's get started," I said.

We collected stones and concrete blocks, sticks and clods of dirt to make the breakfront. Soon we had a pretty good-size wall going. It wouldn't be a comfortable night's sleep, but at least we'd make it through to the morning.

I tried channeling some of my electricity into the pieces of wood we'd gathered. I held my hands over the sticks, palms out. I concentrated, focusing my attention. At first nothing happened at all. But then a small, happy orange flame licked out from the pile of kindling. It was joined by others, and before we knew it, we had a real fire going.

"Just in time," I muttered. "I could barely feel my hands anymore."

Ashley moved in closer to the flames. She peered up at the column of smoke rising against the night sky. "Maybe Ethan will see it," she said, looking wistful, "and come find us."

*I hope so*, I added silently, doubtfully.

Ethan was gone. So was the alien ship, which, for all we knew, was our only way back. Now we were truly stranded. On this horrible planet of the future. Alone.

*Well, not completely alone*, I reminded myself, remembering the killer eyeball.

# Chapter 3

# Ethan

It was the smell that woke me up.

For a full minute I just lay in bed, head on my pillow, afraid to open my eyes. The last time I had awakened to this smell, it was to find a dead, chewed-up mouse lying right beside my face. A present courtesy of our family's cat, Heimlich. Mom said it was just his way of showing he liked me.

If that was the case, I think I was about to see how Heimlich showed he *loved* me.

This smell was *way* worse than the mouse had been. What had Heimlich left this time? A dead squirrel? A bird? Something worse?

Finally I cracked open my eyelids. It was pitch-black in my bedroom. And cold. *Real* cold.

I guess it didn't help that I'd kicked my blankets off in the night. To top it off, something was wrong with the mattress. It was much harder than usual. Plus the pillow was all sticky and furry and—

"*Yeeeuuuuggh!*"

Before the scream escaped my lips, I was on my feet, wide awake, doing a mad little jig like a grossed-out leprechaun. I jumped from foot to foot, swiping frantically at the side of my face with my hands, shaking out my hair, and spitting as if I'd just tasted poison.

Because in that fraction of a second it had all come rushing back to me:

The time machine. The wasteland. Being chased by that floating metal ball that shot lasers. I flashed back to the memory:

*It was after me. Right on my tail. I could hear the weird, high whine of its motor, like an evil dentist's drill. It made me run faster.*

*Up ahead I could see the bombed-out shell of an old building. Crumbling walls, exposed girders. If I made it there, I could maybe find a hiding spot. Something to crawl behind. A way to escape.*

*I was almost there. Another twenty yards.*

*The sun was low, at my back. I was running east. As I ran I could see my shadow, arms pumping, projected on the wall ahead of me.*

*And I could see its shadow. Above mine. A large black disk, just ten feet above me. Hanging in the sky like a deadly black moon.*

*I could practically feel its laser sights locking right between my shoulder blades. It made the skin there prickle. My legs strained, my sneakers pounded on the rocky ground—*

*And then they were pedaling against nothing but air. The ground had disappeared. I pitched forward, thrown off balance, and it was suddenly dark and I was falling, falling. . . .*

17

Now I raised my hand to the back of my head and felt a huge bump underneath my hair. Yikes. No wonder I had thought I was in my bedroom before. I'd obviously had a few screws knocked loose. From the size of the lump, it was a wonder I could still remember my name.

I winced, squeezing my eyes shut as hard as I could. Not because I was in pain. But because I wanted to activate my thermal vision.

When I opened my eyes, things were looking a little brighter. That's not to say things looked *good*, just that they were more brightly lit.

With my thermal vision I can see anything that emits heat. It's kind of hard to describe. But it's pretty cool. Heat looks whitish blue to me, almost like static on a TV. The hotter something is, the brighter it appears.

I was at the bottom of a pit, about eight feet in diameter and fifteen feet deep. It was too perfectly round to have been formed naturally. Someone had dug it.

At first I thought that there was someone lying near my feet. Then I realized it was just my own "heat print," the mark my body heat had left on the ground where I was sleeping. It looked like a glowing blue shadow. I could clearly make out the feet, legs, arms—

I gulped.

Sure enough, what I had initially thought was a pillow was actually the dead body of an animal. I knew it was dead because, aside from the bluish imprint where my head had rested on it (man, did I want a shampoo now), its body was dark and cold.

18

What was it? I wondered. It looked large enough to be a dog, but something told me it wasn't. And I wasn't about to play junior biologist.

Instead I decided to play escape artist. I flattened my back against the side of the pit, spreading out my arms and bracing my hands against the curve in the pit's wall. Exerting all the pressure I could outward against my palms, I slowly managed to lift myself up a few feet.

At first my hands slipped against the smooth surface, and I had to scrabble for a purchase in the dirt with my sneakers. But finally I started to get the hang of it. Soon I was climbing like a human fly.

It wasn't until I was at the top of the pit that I heard it.

*Eeeep . . . eeeep . . . eeeep . . . eeeep . . .*

It was an electronic sound. A beeping. Braced twelve feet above the pit floor, I craned my neck, peering over the lip of the pit. When I found where the noise was coming from, I wished I hadn't.

Because not twenty yards away stood an alien.

Even in the low light, its features were unmistakable. The thin, bony frame. The silvery white skin. The large, bulbous head. And the eyes—two dark, horrible disks that seemed to radiate with evil. In the past, when they had come after us, the aliens were always dressed as the humans they impersonated. But this alien was dressed in its own clothes: a shiny black uniform that stood in stark contrast against its pale skin.

The alien was carrying a small handheld device studded with greenish yellow lights. The mechanism beeped as he scanned the area before him. When he pointed it in my direction, the beeping grew more insistent, like a radar detector picking up a highway cop.

The alien started heading straight toward me.

I ducked my head down, holding on for all I was worth.

*Eeep . . . eeep . . . eeep! Eeep! Eeep!*

The beeps were growing louder and more frequent. He must have been very close to the pit, possibly mere feet away. I didn't dare sneak a peek. My arms were trembling from the strain of holding me in place. Even in the bitter cold, sweat rolled down my forehead. I wasn't going to be able to hold on much longer. I struggled to keep my breath steady and silent.

*Eep! Eep! Eep! Eep! Eep! Eep!*

I heard footsteps only inches from my head, felt them vibrate through my arms. If the alien didn't see me by now, he could probably smell me. Just as I was getting ready to battle to the death . . .

*EEP-EEP-EEP-EEP-EEE—*

. . . the beeping stopped, and the machine snapped off.

I had the horrible sensation that if I tilted up my head, I would come face-to-face with the alien, grinning down at me.

Then I heard the footsteps walk away. I was too tired to hang on any longer. I pulled myself over the lip of the pit and propped myself up on my elbows. From my new perspective I could see the aliens—there were two of them—standing next to what looked like Luke's hover-craft from *Star Wars* crossed with a Jet Ski. The vehicle floated a few feet above the ground. Beneath it the air looked distorted, rippling, the way heat looks as it rises.

"We don't have time," one was saying. "We have new orders that we must act on immediately."

"But I have a bio reading in this sector," the one with the tracking device said.

"It's probably just vermin," the first one replied.

*Vermin?* Suddenly I realized who my bunk buddy had been. Make that *what* it had been. At least Jack would be impressed. It was another one for the record books: World's Largest Rodent.

"Our orders are clear," the alien continued. "'Return to sector Beta—'"

"But this reading is too large for vermin."

"Let me finish. 'Return to sector Beta-3. Respond to *a class-four thermal reading.*'"

"The fools lit a fire!"

"That's right," his companion replied. "We must hurry before they realize their mistake."

They climbed on the hover scooter. Then, with the barely discernable rev of a motor, it was gone.

If the "fools" were who I thought, then my friends were in danger. Worse, they were sitting ducks. I had to warn them.

With the last of my strength I hauled the rest of my body out of the hole.

Rising to my feet, I strained to hear over the high wind, frantically scanning from left to right with my heat vision. There was nothing but darkness.

I started running after the aliens.

I felt helpless. Panicky. But I knew I had to do something.

I hadn't gone fifty yards when I saw something that scared me right out of my pants.

A figure was standing in front of me, perfectly motionless except for its long, ragged overcoat, which flapped in the wind like a shredded flag. Its outstretched arms weren't even of the same length. Its head was bizarre and misshapen, like an overgrown peanut topped with a sloppy felt hat. I couldn't see any legs.

It looked like a giant rag doll or else a poorly made scarecrow.

As I moved closer I started to breathe easier. The "peanut head" was made out of a burlap sack.

*Ethan, you noodlehead. It is a scarecrow.*

But why was there a scarecrow in the middle of this barren plain? *Think, Ethan,* I told myself. *If someone puts up a scarecrow, it must be to guard something. But what? And who are they guarding it from?*

I stepped right up to the scarecrow, inspecting it for any clues. Then the totally unexpected happened.

It grabbed me.

# Chapter 4

# Jack

"It grabbed me," I told Ashley, who was sitting at the edge of the campfire, paralyzed with fear, "and started dragging me down into the grave. I struggled, but I couldn't get away. Its bony hand was wrapped too tightly around my ankle."

"I thought the killer had a hook," Ashley cut in.

"He *did* have a hook," I replied. "On his *other* hand. Don't interrupt."

"Jack," Toni said groggily, starting to wake up, "stop telling Ashley ghost stories and try to get some sleep."

"Gee," I answered, "since when were you my mother?"

Ashley suddenly bolted upright. "Guys, do you hear that?" she asked.

This time we knew better than to ignore her. "Hear what, Ash? What does it sound like?"

"Like footsteps," she replied. "Someone is coming."

"Maybe it's Ethan," Toni suggested.

We all fell silent.

I scanned the darkness, trying to keep my nerves under control. Everywhere I looked, I thought I could see another figure hiding in the shadows, picked out by the flickering light of the fire. My heart started to go ballistic. *Okay, Jack,* I told myself. *It's probably just Ethan. And he's probably not even undead, or carrying a hook for a hand, or—*

Just then—there—at the edge the circle formed by the light of our dying fire appeared a kid wearing some kind of fur caveman costume straight out of *The Flintstones*. He looked about ten or eleven, and he was pointing what looked like a homemade crossbow directly at us.

"Why don't you put that thing away," I suggested, "before electric girl here decides to short your circuits?"

Toni shot me a dirty look. I could see she was trying to do just that—muster up an electric charge—but it didn't look like she had enough juice.

"Don't move," Cave Boy said through clenched teeth. "Don't even breathe."

"I'm serious, dude. You don't want to get on her bad side," I replied. "Do you like our fire? If you're nice to us, we can show you how to build one of your very own."

"I said *don't move*," he growled, even more fiercely. Then without warning he let the arrow fly.

For a second I thought it was all over. But the missile didn't hit me.

I actually heard a *hissss!* as it passed right by my ear, a *chthunk!* as it sank deep into the flesh of something right behind me, then the most horrible shrieking I have ever heard in my life.

I whirled around to see what was there . . . and came face-to-face with a hideous creature about the size of a well-fed Saint Bernard. As I watched, it tumbled onto its

24

back, clawing at the arrow in its throat. Its cries were like the squeal of a drowning pig, a combination growl and gargle. After a moment it lay still, its mouth open, its sharp teeth gleaming in the firelight. Only its long rodent's tail still lashed back and forth, like a large pink snake. Then finally the tail stopped, too.

It was a rat. A giant mutant rat.

Another second and it would have gotten me. One look at those massive teeth told me that I wouldn't have lasted long.

"Hey . . . thanks," I told Cave Boy. "That was close."

"*Close?*" Toni repeated. "That was more like right on top of you."

"What's your name?" Ashley asked the boy, who was already loading a new arrow into his crossbow. "Are you out here by yourself?"

He didn't even seem to hear what she was saying. He strode quickly to the fire and began kicking sand and loose dirt over the burning wood.

"Um, is there a reason you're putting out our only means of survival?" Toni asked. "Doesn't that seem a little *counterproductive?*"

The kid didn't answer.

"*Counterproductive* is a vocabulary word," Toni went on. "It means—"

"I know what it means," he told her. "But we don't have time to talk. They know you're here. They'll be coming any second."

"Who?" Ashley asked. "Who will be coming?"

The boy looked up. "The Omegas," he said.

It wasn't what he said. It was the way he said it. That was all it took. We were up on our feet, kicking dirt on the flames.

In a few seconds the last glowing ember was extinguished. Only a thin column of smoke rose into the dark sky. As soon as the wind picked up again, that would be gone, too.

The kid was bent over the dead body of the rat, unfolding a large burlap sack. "Help me," he said. "I can't lift the rat all by myself."

Toni looked down at him. "Are you sure you want to take the rat?" she asked. "It looks awfully heavy. Won't it, like, slow us down?"

The boy just looked up at her, still trying to lift the rat corpse. I knew the look in his eyes. "She asks a lot of questions," I told him. "Don't worry, you'll get used to it. Here. I'll help you."

I grabbed the back legs of the rat creature while he held open the mouth of the sack. Between the two of us we managed to get it in the bag.

"Now what?" Toni asked when we were finished, looking even more annoyed than usual. "Do we wrap it and put a bow on top?"

"Now we flee," Cave Boy told her. Then he looked at me. "You are the biggest. You carry the rat," he said. "Hurry."

I thought I heard Toni's giggling as I strained under the weight of the dead rat. It was going to be slow going. *Why wasn't I the one with superstrength?* I wondered for the millionth time.

I struggled to keep up.

26

# Chapter 5

# Ashley

My mind was racing. So Metier was inhabited after all—the wild boy who had come to our rescue was proof! Maybe there had been other survivors, too.

*But survivors of what?* I wondered. *What happened to my hometown? And when?*

Our guide practically ran through the burned-out rubble, even though it was too dark to see. The city ruins were like an obstacle course. We twisted and turned through tight passageways, ducked under and dodged past barriers that seemed to appear out of nowhere. Toni held my hand as we ran. I could hear Jack's labored breathing as he dragged the rat's carcass behind us.

Or at least I hoped it was Jack's.

Suddenly I became aware of a faint buzzing noise off in the distance. It was the same humming I'd heard earlier, right before the attack. "Hey," I called to our guide, "there's something coming." What had he called them again? "Omegas."

The boy put his ear to the ground. "Not Omegas," he announced. "Sweepers."

"Sweepers, Omegas," Jack said, "we're getting all the new vocabulary words today. Toni should be happy."

"They're still a long way off," the boy continued. He rose, unfastening a small leather pouch from his belt. "We can set a decoy. You," he said, pointing to Jack, "put down the rat."

Jack dropped the rat to the ground with a thud. "Gee," he panted, "are you sure? I was really starting to enjoy carrying it."

The boy removed a plastic bottle from his pouch. It was filled with a thin, yellowish liquid. He unscrewed the cap and turned it over the sack. The oily liquid sloshed out.

"Gasoline," Toni said, crinkling her nose.

"When I tell you to, run," the boy said. "Not a moment sooner."

"Or what?" Toni asked, clearly none too happy about being bossed around by an eleven-year-old.

"Or you will be blown into a thousand charred bits," he replied.

"Oh," Toni said. "Okay."

The humming was much louder by now. "They're almost here," I told the boy. "Are you sure you know what you're doing?"

He said nothing, only watched the horizon. "Get ready. Don't run till I say 'go.' Whatever you do, don't stop."

That was when we saw them. They came speeding over the horizon like a cluster of angry, silver bees. There were five of them this time—"Sweepers"—just like the one that chased Ethan. They were headed straight for us.

"When I say 'go,'" the boy repeated, as if he were trying to hypnotize us, "run." He had removed two rocks from his belt pouch. "Ready . . . set . . ."

The Sweepers were now less than fifty feet away. You didn't need superhearing to hear their laser guns charging.

"Come *on*, let's *go*," said Toni. I could hear the fear in her voice.

"Not yet," the boy said, "almost there . . . almost there . . ."

The Sweepers' metal eyelids opened. Their red eyes locked focus.

"This is crazy," I blurted. "We have to run—"

"*Now!*" yelled the small boy. He brought the two rocks together with a grinding swipe, sending a shower of tiny white sparks onto the gasoline-soaked burlap sack.

*Fooom!*

I turned and ran as hard as I could, the hard, flat ground slapping against the soles of my boots, the cold night air tearing at my lungs. At any moment I expected to feel the searing pain of a laser slice through my shoulder blades. Or at the very least to hear one of my friends cry out in pain as the Sweepers cut them down beside me.

To my amazement, it didn't happen. Finally we reached a small rise where a large concrete water pipe lay exposed. We climbed onto it, then slid down the other side. Miraculously we were all there—and unhurt.

"They're buying it," the boy said. "We're safe."

In the distance we could see the cluster of evil metal orbs hovering over the burning corpse of our rat. They jostled in place, as if uncertain what to do next.

"The rat is the right size and shape to be their target," the boy told us. "But they know that something isn't right, so they're going in for a closer look. And that's where they make their mistake."

As we watched, one of the orbs fired its laser cannon, seemingly at random. Then another one fired straight up, the laser beam piercing the blackness above.

"Their sensors aren't equipped to deal with that kind of direct heat," the boy explained. "It makes them kind of crazy. The next thing you know, they're all shooting each other up."

Another Sweeper fired, this time scoring a direct hit— on a fellow Sweeper. Crippled and dying, the wounded Sweeper returned fire, with fatal results. Soon the night was filled with the rapid flashes of laser fire, like photographers snapping photos of a celebrity. When it was over, five metal shells lay smoldering on the ground.

"It only works once per sector," the boy continued, "then they figure it out. We got lucky."

"You're not kidding," Jack replied. "First we were almost rat food, then we almost got cut to pieces by the Evil Eyes. You saved our lives twice in a half hour, and we don't even know your name."

"It's Whistler," the boy replied. "At least that's what I'm called."

"I'm Ashley," I told him. "Thank you for what you did."

"It's my pleasure, Ashley," he responded, smiling.

"I'm Antonia," Toni said. "My friends call me Toni."

"Hi, Toni," the boy told her.

"My name is Danger," Jack said.

Whistler looked confused. "Danger?" he asked.

"Forget it," Jack muttered. "You can call me Jack."

"I was out hunting when I saw your fire," Whistler told us. "It is a very bad idea to light a fire. Heat is what attracts the Sweepers." Then he thought for a moment. "On the other hand, it's a good thing you *did* light a fire because if you *hadn't* and I hadn't seen you, you'd be rat food." He frowned. "Life is full of paradoxes."

"You're pretty deep," Toni said. "For someone who wears fur."

"Are there others around here who are, you know, like us?" Jack asked. "I mean, not made out of metal and not giant rats?"

"Sure," he said. "Would you like to meet them?"

"Very much," I assured him.

"Then follow me," he said. "I am a good guide."

I couldn't believe our luck. Narrowly escaping death not once but twice. Instead of freezing to death or starving, we were going to be taken to meet other humans and find shelter. Maybe we'd finally find out what happened to Metier.

*And maybe*, a little voice sang out inside me, *we'll find Ethan.*

The course Whistler led us on was a giant maze. Sometimes we were scurrying over the surface, darting from the shattered remains of one long-dead building to another. Other times we were on our hands and knees, crawling through tunnels deep under the ground or running through empty sewer pipes, crouched over double so that we wouldn't bump our heads.

Finally we emerged before a big pile of debris. "We're here," Whistler announced, pointing at the rubble. There, embedded in a block of pockmarked concrete, was a set of double doors. "It's a tunnel," Whistler explained, "that leads to headquarters."

Each of the tarnished brass doors had fancy raised letters on them—*LH*. I knew instantly where I'd seen them before. We were standing at the site of the old Liberty Hotel. Whistler's "tunnel" was actually the hotel's elevator—or at least it had been.

The year I turned four, my parents took me to the Liberty Hotel to meet the Easter Bunny. The mall hadn't even been built yet. Everyone was dressed for the holiday: All the women were in big, beautiful hats and spring dresses, and the men were in suits. Back then, Liberty Hotel was the most elegant place in town. I remember thinking that it was just like a palace.

Now it was nothing but a few hunks of marble and concrete.

Whistler pried open the doors of the elevator, exposing a dark shaft heading down into the ground. There didn't seem to be anything inside at all. I had no idea how he expected us to get down it, but I hoped it didn't involve jumping or climbing.

Suddenly Whistler brought one hand up to his mouth and stuck several fingers inside. *Gross,* I thought, going over the list of things he'd touched in the last hour, which included a huge dead rat and the inside of a sewer pipe. Whistler blew hard through his fingers. The noise was truly mind warping. It was less a whistle than a sonic blast. The ball of sound echoed around in the darkness before it finally disappeared.

"That's how I got my name," he said, grinning at us bashfully.

"I'm glad your name isn't Farter," Jack said.

From inside the dark shaft we heard the sound of a rusty wheel turning and squeaking under the strain of something heavy. A pulley system. Slowly a wooden platform rose into view, with a gangly boy about Whistler's age on it, holding a thick rope. He nodded at Whistler, who nodded back.

"Come on," Whistler told us, "let's go."

We got on the thin plank of wood. Then the big brass doors closed, shutting out the howling wind and plunging us into total darkness. With Whistler's help Pulley Boy began our hand-over-hand descent down the old elevator shaft. Above us the metal wheel groaned like a mournful ghost as we were lowered into the unknown.

# Chapter 6

# Ethan

*"Unnnhhhhhhhh . . ."*

When I came to, I heard a long, low groan. Someone was in serious pain.

And then I realized that someone was *me*.

My head still throbbed with a dull ache. Just like when I woke up down in the pit, only worse. I was pretty sure there was a new bump on my old bump. What had happened *this* time?

Gradually the fog lifted from my memory: what had happened was the *scarecrow*—that creepy guy in the tattered duds with the burlap sack over his head.

My eyes fluttered open. At first I couldn't see anything, then my thermal vision focused on the tiny thatchwork of rough material an inch in front of my face.

Apparently I'd been given a burlap sack of my very own. The coarse fabric was dry and dusty. It made my eyes itch and filled my nostrils with rank, moldy air.

I didn't know what time it was, but I figured I'd been out cold for a while. The material under my cheek was damp from where I'd drooled on it in my sleep.

I tried to sit up, to move my hands, only to find they were bound tightly behind my back.

And I was moving. Moving fast.

Someone was pushing me from behind in some kind of rickety old shopping cart or wheelbarrow. If it really was a scarecrow come to life, he definitely wasn't taking me on the Yellow Brick Road. This road was unpaved, with more bumps and ruts than the Oregon Trail. My body rattled and banged hard against the metal sides of the moving cage.

"Hey!" I finally shouted. "Let me out of here!"

"Quiet," a voice behind me rasped. "Or the next whack on the head will be twice as hard."

"Where are you taking me?" I asked, trying a calmer tone.

"To market," the voice said.

"Market?"

"That's right. It's the third sun cycle of the lunar quarter. Time to go to the market."

"In other words, it's Wednesday."

"Wednesday?" he echoed, bewildered. "What's Wednesday?"

*Gee. A lot more than buildings and the ozone layer got obliterated,* I thought as I continued to be pushed along like a bag of groceries toward some checkout lane in hell.

About twenty minutes and ten thousand bumps later the cart finally rattled to a halt.

"Here we are," announced my captor, almost with glee, as he dumped me out onto the ground.

He yanked the bag from my head and I sucked in the air, gasping with relief. It was polluted air, but anything was better than the inside of that bag.

35

"Get on your feet," he commanded.

Weak from my long, torturous ride, I had some trouble getting up. My knees were still shaking badly.

"Stand up straight!" he ordered. "Look alive! It's show time!"

I turned around to get a better look at my captor and drill sergeant.

*Whoa*, I thought, nearly jumping back.

Even though he wore that canvas sack over his head, there were enough slits and holes in it to see his face underneath. And it wasn't pretty.

Talk about a dermatologist's nightmare. His cheeks were a horrifying patchwork of burned and scarred tissue. His lips—well, he didn't have any. His mouth was just a hollow void where maybe a half dozen rotten teeth dangled like tiny Christmas ornaments. Plaque was the least of his worries.

His hands seemed more like claws—covered by ratty old socks, with just the gnarled thumb and index fingers exposed. And speaking of ratty, his long fur coat was *truly* ratty. As in made of stitched-together rat pelts.

In short, he was a cross between Spawn—without his mask—and Scarecrow, one of the Batman villains. Or maybe a combination of Freddy Krueger and Dark Man. Whatever he was, he couldn't possibly be human. No way. *Hobo sapiens* was more like it.

We were standing outside a sprawling building that I recognized as the old indoor rink for the Metier Meteorites hockey team. It had seen better times. What used to be the parking lot was now a bubbling cesspool. It surrounded the old arena like a protective moat around a castle.

I had hardly had time to wonder how people got across when a voice began whining to my right. "Entry fee! Entry fee!"

A tiny man, less than four feet tall, was hobbling over to us. He, too, was a hideous sight, covered in an odd outfit of rags and rodent pelts. "What do you have for me today, Daggs?" he asked.

"How's this?" the scarecrow—apparently named Daggs—said, holding something up.

"Hey, that's my watch!" I protested, recognizing the Seiko I'd gotten for my thirteenth birthday.

Daggs shoved me backward to the ground. I was suddenly eye level with the guard. "Stay out of this," Daggs warned me.

The guard snatched my watch from Daggs with a scowl and tossed it onto a large pile of other items apparently collected as an "entry fee." There were strange-looking bones, rusted hubcaps, ashtrays, a candelabra, umbrellas. . . . I even saw an old copy of *TV Guide* with George Clooney on the cover.

Satisfied, the guard put two fingers in his mouth and delivered a series of long and short whistles. Moments later a drawbridge made of welded-together scraps of metal was lowered from the other side. It looked way too flimsy and weak to support us.

"You go first," Daggs ordered. "The two of us on it together will be too much weight."

So I went first—very carefully—my hands still tied behind my back. The cesspool below me spewed and swelled like red-hot lava, sending up wispy white fumes that stung my eyes and nearly made me gag.

"Hurry, boy!" Daggs yelled. "The market doesn't stay open forever!"

I picked up my pace. But midway across I tripped on a loose plank, falling to my knees and nearly slipping into the caustic muck.

Daggs stormed across the bridge himself and with one clawlike hand reached down and pulled me back up onto my feet. "I knew you'd bring me nothing but trouble!" he growled in my ear. "Should just let you fall in and be done with you, you worthless nillibut!"

Muttering more obscenities, Daggs shoved me forward until we made it to the other side.

I had a feeling the Metier Meteorites weren't playing hockey today.

Once inside the huge arena, I found myself amid a raging sea of even more freakish humanoids. All of them were hunched over and badly deformed like Daggs. Some even worse.

Since we were now under a protective roof, many of them chose not to wear a sack over their head. (Thankfully, Daggs kept his on.) It was like a giant mutant convention. Or a Halloween party where everyone was dressed as the same monster.

They buzzed with excitement as they stood over long

tables and shelves of items up for sale or barter. Above them thick cargo netting had been strung about ten feet off the ground. It stretched from one end of the old hockey rink to the other, like a giant spiderweb. Some goods were stowed above it, and even more items dangled from this makeshift ceiling.

Judging from the merchandise, these freaks were into their rat wear. You could find any piece of clothing, from coats and hats to skirts, woven out of the rodents' hides.

We passed a stand where some of the female mutants were trying on bizarre wigs made of what looked like dirty straw and hairbrush bristles. One was trying on an old mop head, the same kind Mr. Dailey, our school janitor, used whenever someone puked in the lunchroom. Heck, maybe it *was* the same one.

There were some who scratched their leathery chins as they considered fake limbs and face shields made from old soda cans and recycled tinfoil. I spotted one guy staring curiously at an old CD box of the Spice Girls' first album. Another held up a badly worn pair of sneakers to see if they matched his foot size.

As Daggs pushed me forward through the teeming throng I noticed that most of them didn't just look at me. They *stared* at me, each muttering something under their breath.

One old hag with an eye patch approached and pulled me back by the hair for a closer inspection. She sized me up with her one good eye and asked, "How much for one of his ogglers, Daggzie?"

"Too much for you, Cora," Daggs growled. "Shove off."

A towering goon who was missing a nose bent down and squeezed mine—as if he were feeling a tomato for ripeness.

"Back away, Argus," Daggs snapped. "You'll get a chance to make a bid soon enough! Now let us through!"

Argus reluctantly gave in and let us pass. But more of the crowd continued to follow closely behind us.

I just looked straight ahead, trying to avoid their creepy stares and openmouthed gawks.

*What did Daggs mean by 'make a bid'? What exactly is going on here?*

My answer came about twenty feet later.

A row of ten Toledo scales lined the back wall of the old hockey rink. Men and women who looked fairly normal—more human than humanoid, that is—were forced to step up and be weighed. Like me, their hands were tied behind their backs. Some were wearing leg irons.

When Daggs pushed me toward one of the open scales, several mutants who were ready to bid on the others rushed over to me. "Daggs!" one shouted. "Where did you find such a perfect specimen as that?"

"I'll give you a thousand right now, Daggs," another one said. "No questions asked."

"Get away!" Daggs barked. "All of you! We're gonna do this thing proper. Highest bidder takes him, and that's that. Now give me room!"

The whole place immediately fell quiet as they waited

for me to step up onto the Toledo scale. Daggs pulled my T-shirt off over my head. It fell down over my bound wrists.

All at once the whispering began. I caught snatches of their awed conversations.

"Look at him. . . ."

"A perfect specimen . . ."

"Oh, what I'd give to have that skin . . . that beautiful, uncontaminated hide!"

Then Daggs pushed me onto the scale. Everyone watched wide-eyed as the needle zoomed past 105, wavered a bit, then stopped dead on 102.

"One . . . oh . . . two!" a mutant cried out. "One! Oh! Two!"

That number rippled through the sea of freaks like a magic number to be recorded for the rest of time. They said it over and over again, their voices echoing.

Daggs pulled me down off the scale. He then climbed onto a wooden crate and lifted me up next to him. "I'm starting the bidding at twelve hundred," he announced with an air of smugness. Apparently I wasn't such a worthless "nillibut" after all.

At first he was answered with a wave of gasps and protests. Then someone from the back shouted out: "Two thousand!"

"Twenty-one hundred!" another countered.

"Twenty-four!" someone else yelled.

"Twenty-six!"

The bidding soared as the wealthier mutants came out

of the woodwork. Daggs must have been glowing inside his burlap bag.

"Three thousand," a woman called out.

I had to free my hands somehow. To get out of there. To save my hide—literally—before it became someone's new face.

"Thirty-five hundred!"

As the bidding accelerated, so did my adrenaline. It began to pulse through my veins in double time. My senses grew ultraheightened. I could see everything clearly and in zoomlike close-up. The shouts and murmurs of the multitude became silent in my ears. My whole body just relaxed—from the ends of my toes to the tips of my fingers.

I could feel the power of myself fill up within me. The strength felt endless. It felt good.

As my focus on escape intensified, the rope around my wrists gradually loosened. And loosened some more. I tugged at the knot, and it unraveled like a bow on a gift box.

I looked over at Daggs, and my fear of him was completely gone. I almost wanted to laugh.

Then I peered up at the cargo netting suspended above me. From atop the crate it was only about three feet out of reach. Through its wide webbing I could just make out the old arena scoreboard high up in the shadows. The rusty display still had the final score of the very last game played here: Metier 3, Beloit 3.

It was time for Ethan Rogers to break the tie and win

one for the home team. It was time for Ethan Rogers to kick some serious mutant butt.

"Hey, Daggzie," I said. "I got a joke for you."

My calm, friendly tone must have thrown him. He looked down at me, scowling under his foul headgear. "Be quiet, or I'll sell you limb by limb," he threatened as he tried to keep track of the frenzied bidding. By now it was over five thousand.

"What did the woman say to her mutant husband?" I pressed on.

His eyes widened at my question.

"I'd kiss you . . . but I *just ate*," I said, punctuating the punch line with an uppercut to his burlapped face. He flew off the crate and hit the floor with a dull thud.

I jumped up and grabbed hold of the cargo netting.

"Get him!" someone snarled. And the excited crowd became an unruly mob.

I moved swiftly above their heads along the cargo net—at first crawling like Spidey, then swinging Tarzan style from hand to hand. The stronger, younger mutants followed me below. One jumped up at my ankles, nearly pulling me loose. But I wriggled out of his grasp.

"You can't escape!" one mutant yelled.

"There's no way out of here!" another one growled.

Finally I ran out of net. I was up against the Plexiglas barrier that kept the pucks from leaving the rink. Now I knew how the puck felt. I had no choice but to drop back down to the floor. I dropped, spun—

And saw a mutant charging at me with a spear.

With my vision at its most acute, size and motion were distorted in my favor. The spear appeared to be nothing more than a toothpick. His attacking speed seemed like a leisurely gait.

I easily sidestepped him and—*poom!*—delivered a crushing backhand to his neck. He collapsed like a fold-out card table.

And then others followed. I took out one with a roundhouse kick . . . dodged a dagger thrust from another and felled him with an elbow to his one-eyed face. I grabbed the next attacker by the arm and flipped him onto his back. The ensuing *crunch* was not a pretty sound.

But they kept coming. And coming. Three from the front. Two from the side. Two more from the back.

As soon as I would knock out one with a scissors kick another would take his place. Their attack was relentless. They eventually fought me into a corner of the old rink.

I was running out of room. I was running out of breath.

After another head butt and jab that took out two more mutants, another one jumped on me from out of nowhere. He caught my left arm with a broken bottle before I was able to shake him off into another attacker.

And then the strangest thing happened.

The mutants suddenly stopped their assault. Instead they just stood there in a semicircle around me, their horrible mouths gaping in awe.

*Gosh. Was it something I said?*

"Another silverblood!" one finally proclaimed, pointing excitedly at my left arm.

I looked down. My left arm was bleeding. Silver blood. "He's one for the Fight!" someone else cried.

"Yes!" others agreed. "He's a silverblood—he must be saved for the pit!".

Another mutant broke through the front line. I didn't recognize him without his canvas mask. His exposed burned face contorted into a hideous, lipless smile.

"Yes, he must fight," he said. "But just remember one thing. This silverblood still belongs to *me*. . . ."

Before I could move a muscle, they were on me.

# Chapter 7

## Toni

As soon as we reached the bottom of the elevator shaft we were greeted by four big guys dressed in tight-fitting leather vests and pants to match. Of course, their idea of a "greeting" was to point crossbows at us similar to the one Whistler had used to shoot the mutant rat. Except that if Whistler's was the hunting model, these were designed for all-out warfare. The gleaming point aimed directly at my throat looked like it could have pierced a concrete-reinforced wall . . . and kept on going.

"Take it easy!" I managed to squeak out. "Whistler, do you know these guys?"

Without saying a word, Whistler flashed the guards a series of complex hand signals. They immediately lowered their weapons, still looking about as friendly as stone statues.

"Pretty cool," Jack told Whistler. "Is there another signal you can do to make them dance?"

"Never mind Jack," I said, "he was dropped as a baby."

We continued to make our way along the underground passageway, passing through no fewer than four checkpoints like the one we'd just gone through. *Either these guys have something valuable to protect,* I thought, *or there's something out there they really have to protect themselves* from.

The network of tunnels ran through what had once been the basement of the Liberty Hotel, weaving through a series of tiny rooms lit with a mix of candles and small lamps. If you could make a map of the place, I bet it would look like a big ant farm. Still, it was kind of cozy— if you were Yoda or something.

Finally we reached our destination: a big room built in what had once been the hotel's Olympic-size swimming pool. A huge oak table stretched from one end of the room to the other. The walls were lined with thousands upon thousands of books in tall shelves. More stacks of books, rolled-up maps, and piles of papers littered the floor. Enormous, wax-dripping chandeliers added to the light from the dozens of candles scattered around the room.

"Professor!" Whistler shouted out as we entered, his voice echoing off the tiles in the vaultlike chamber. "I've brought visitors! From Topside."

"Topside?" Ashley whispered to me, raising one eyebrow.

"And who have you brought to us now, Whistler, my boy?" asked a white-haired, white-bearded man who stepped out from behind a shelf, a pile of books under one arm. He reminded me of a poster of Albert Einstein that hung in Mr. Holland's science lab: *186,000 miles per second—it's not just a good idea, it's the law.* He had the same bushy eyebrows and wild hairstyle.

Whistler pointed to us proudly. "I found them while I was hunting."

Placing his books down on the table, the white-haired man stepped over to us. He moved from Ashley to Jack to me, peering closely at each of us over his glasses, like a jeweler examining a gemstone for flaws. "And you are certain they're not Omega spies?" he asked, lifting my chin and staring intensely in my eyes.

Whistler looked uncomfortable. "Well . . . I didn't do the test. But trust me. They're too stupid to be Omegas. They were nearly killed by the rats after they lit a fire."

"Stupid?" Jack muttered. "And just how many languages can *you* speak, Mowgli?"

"Even so," the professor said, taking one of my hands gently in his own, "we can't be too careful, you know." He examined the back of my hand, then turned it over.

For a second I thought maybe the old guy was going to read my palm. Then his grip unexpectedly grew tight around my wrist. With his other hand he reached into the pocket of his trousers and withdrew a long, wicked-looking razor. It was caked with rust, gleaming dully in the candlelight.

He brought the rusty blade to my palm. I was too shocked even to scream.

"Hey, Doc!" Jack cried, coming to my rescue. He grabbed the old man's wrist, stopping him from cutting me. "Unless you've also got a tetanus shot in that pocket, I think you're about to make a *mondo* medical no-no."

"I'll say!" I screeched. I had finally found my voice. And it was a good two octaves above my regular one.

"But it's the rule," the old man replied. "It's the only

way we can be sure you're not the enemy. The only—"

Right then, without warning, the ground lurched and Jack, the professor, and I went crashing to the floor. The old man's razor spun away across the tiles, which were heaving like the deck of a ship in a storm.

"Quake!" Whistler yelled over a thunderous rumbling.

Ashley stood frozen in place, somehow keeping her balance as one of the tall wooden bookcases teetered precariously behind her. It was going to crush her.

"Ashley!" I screamed from the floor. "Look out!" But my voice was lost in the roar.

A split second before Ashley would have become library paste, Whistler dove at her, pushing her out of the way. The shelf crashed to the floor with a sickening, bone-crunching *crack!*

And then—just like that—it was over.

The whole earthquake had lasted fifteen seconds, tops. Now the only sounds were the slight creaking of the ropes that supported the two swinging chandeliers. Remarkably, a few of the candles in them were still lit, glowing brightly in the plaster dust that clouded the air.

"Is everyone okay?" Whistler asked.

"I think so," Jack replied.

"Well," I said as the professor and I got back to our feet, "I guess you can get back to slicing me open now."

This time it was Ashley who came to my rescue. "You guys . . . ," she said. Something about her voice made us all turn and pay attention.

Ashley was sitting cross-legged on the floor, in the

middle of a mess of books and papers from the over-turned bookcase. She was holding a photograph in her hand. "Look at this."

We walked over to her.

It was a group photo of eight adults—five men and three women, standing in a line. They all wore the same strange uniform: a dark blue jumpsuit, kind of like astronauts wear. No one in the picture was smiling. There was a date at the bottom: January 16, 2089.

Ashley's hand was shaking as she pointed out one of the figures—a tall woman with long, curly brown hair. "That's my mother," Ashley said.

Jack reached over and pointed to another person in the photo, a redheaded man with a mustache. "And that's my dad."

The two of them looked at me expectantly.

My eyes had already locked on a third figure in the photograph. An attractive African American woman with kind, almond-shaped eyes. I swallowed hard. "That's her, all right," I said.

The professor took the photo from Ashley's hand. He looked at it, then back at us, with a stunned expression on his face.

"The Alpha children," the professor whispered. "Henley said you might come."

# Chapter 8

# Jack

It was a long story, but the professor wanted to hear every-thing. Somehow we managed to get across the main points of our bizarre tale in record time. Toni and I bickered over the details, but Ashley helped settle any serious disputes.

We were sitting at one end of the long wood table, surrounded by maybe forty of the professor's friends, a mix of adults, teenagers, and younger kids like Whistler. Most of the adult men were wearing the same weird leather vests we'd seen on the guards. Thankfully, they'd left their crossbows at home.

Everyone was staring at us. I couldn't tell whether it was because we were strange, our clothing was strange, or because we were basically doing one big Hoover vacuum imitation on their dinner. But the truth was, I was too hungry to care.

I wolfed down enormous spoonfuls of the thick chicken stew that sat in front of me. It was delicious—like a cross between a sloppy joe without the bread and a bur-rito without the tortilla. Of course, at that point wood shavings would have tasted great.

Toni was the first to remember her manners. She

dabbed at her mouth delicately with a rough cloth napkin and said, "This is the best chicken I've ever had."

"Chicken?" asked the professor, looking confused.

"You know—chicken?" Toni said. "Eats corn, can't fly. A bird?"

"Bird?" the professor asked, looking even more confused.

"Sure, a bird," Toni said. She flapped her arms helpfully.

"Toni," Ashley interrupted, "I don't think this is chicken stew."

"What do you mean?" Toni asked.

"Well, do the math," Ashley replied. "One: Whistler was out *hunting* when he rescued us. Two: He didn't rescue us from a giant mutant *chicken*."

Toni lowered her spoon. "But that doesn't mean—"

"And *three*," Ashley blurted, "*I just found a whisker.*"

"Oh. Ohmigod." Toni looked down at her steaming bowl of stew. She pushed it quickly away from her, then regained her cool. "I think I'm finished," she said, forcing a smile.

"*I'm* not," I shouted. "Second helpings on the rat, please!"

"I don't believe you," Toni said.

"What?" I asked. "It tasted fine when it was chicken, right?"

As I continued to scarf down everything in sight the professor told us what he knew about what had happened to Earth and about our missing parents. It went something like this:

For decades the United States military had been trying

52

to create the ultimate armed forces—the "perfect soldier." By the mid-twenty-first century, scientific advances in genetic engineering made this possible. A process called gene splicing allowed scientists to create a new breed of soldier: humans who were genetically enhanced for survival in hostile climates and armed with specific, superhuman powers. These powers included fighting skills, underwater abilities, communication and spying expertise, even psychic powers.

The first results were the Alphas—the eight men and women in the photo Ashley had found. Our missing parents.

Unfortunately the Alphas weren't the ruthless killing machines that the government had hoped for. The government decided they wanted soldiers who wouldn't think for themselves, who would follow orders blindly and without question.

The Omegas were the government's second batch. Unlike the Alphas, the Omegas didn't have a human conscience and were able to shape-shift to acclimate themselves to any environment—including the nuclear radiation of a postapocalyptic world. What the government didn't realize was how truly ruthless and *inhuman* their creations were. By the time the military officials figured out how much danger they were in, the Omegas had infiltrated the Pentagon and launched a full-scale nuclear war in the year 2094. With their superior resistance to radiation and nuclear fallout, the Omegas were able to rule what was left of the planet.

Fortunately when the war broke out, some people were smart enough to hide in underground fallout shelters—including some right here in Metier. They had been waiting, patiently, for the radiation to die down enough for the surface to be safe again for normal life.

Meanwhile those human survivors foolish enough to stay aboveground were hideously deformed by the radiation. And the worst damage wasn't done to their bodies—it was done to their *minds.* Nuclear fallout and the depletion of the ozone layer accelerated the destruction of their skin, but the outward decay was nothing compared to what happened inside their skulls. They went mad. And so now there was another danger on the surface: a race of subhuman lunatics called Topsiders. They had become relentless skin scavengers—fighting one another for bits and pieces to patch their mutilated bodies.

Over time some of the underground survivors, led by Henley, one of the Alphas, banded together into a movement called the Resistance, with a single mission in mind: to fight the Omegas. But so far they'd had no luck.

"Every time a new base for the Resistance was formed, the Omegas found it." The professor looked deeply sad, probably remembering the friends he lost in the battle.

"How many times have you had to move?" Ashley asked.

"This base is our eleventh base in the seven years since the bombing," he replied. "Ten times the Omegas have destroyed us. So far they haven't located this camp. But how long will it last?"

"Maybe you could convince the Topsiders to join you in your fight," I suggested. "After all, they can't be too happy about the way things turned out."

"We tried that," the professor replied, shaking his head. "Henley, your friend Ethan's father, had that same idea. Three months ago he made a trip to the Topsider camp. It was his intention to form an alliance with the Topsiders, to recruit their help in fighting the Omegas. But he never returned."

"Maybe that's what happened to Ethan," Ashley said. "Perhaps the Topsiders found him and took him to their village."

The professor shook his head sadly. "I'm afraid the best you can hope for is that the rats or Sweepers found him first."

Ashley's eyes flashed with anger. "How can you say that?" she demanded. "Take that back!"

"I say it," the old man replied gently, "because death by rat or Sweeper would at least be swift. If the Topsiders do in fact have your friend, the fate that awaits him is too horrible for words."

Ashley looked like she was torn between wanting to hit someone and wanting to cry. Clearly she wasn't going to take no for an answer—even from someone who seemed to know what he was talking about.

My own mind was troubled by other thoughts. As much as the professor had just cleared up, other questions were still as big a mystery as ever. For example, where did time travel come into it? Why did the Alphas travel into the past and have us kids? Why were the Omegas after us? It didn't make any sense.

My thoughts were interrupted by something I saw at

the other end of the table. It was a little girl sitting in the kiddie section. She had short, flaming red hair that poked out in all directions. She couldn't have been more than six years old. Her bright green eyes were glued on Toni. Or, more specifically, on Toni's gold necklace. She was staring at it hungrily, like a cat eyeing a canary.

The six-year-old caught me looking at her. She scowled and made a face. I made a face back. Then she stuck out her tongue.

Maybe she saw the look in *my* eyes. Maybe she realized her mistake. Or maybe she was just feeling guilty. But before I could say or do a thing, she had ducked under the table and was heading for the door.

There was no time to lose.

I put a hand on Ashley's shoulder. She was still trembling with fear and anger. "It's been a big day," I told the kindly professor. "And that was a great meal. But I'm feeling really beat. Do you mind if I'm excused from the table?"

He smiled and waved his hand. "Go right ahead," he said.

"Suddenly you're polite?" Toni asked me. "That rat stew must have gone bad."

"Follow me," I whispered. "Don't make a scene, just follow me." I leaned in close to Ashley's ear. "You come, too," I told her under my breath.

"Why?" Ashley asked.

"Because I think I've found a clue to where Ethan is," I told her. Then I turned and left the room.

# Chapter 9

# Ashley

After thanking the professor for dinner, Toni and I worked our way along the maze of underground passageways, trying to figure out where Jack had gone. Why had he run off like that? Could he really have a clue as to Ethan's whereabouts?

The idea of finding Ethan gave me butterflies—but that might just have been dinner. I suppose protein is protein (that's what they taught us back in Mr. Holland's biology class, anyway), but the fact that we'd just had a 100 percent rat supper turned my stomach.

For a second I thought we'd lost Jack for good, but then I heard his muffled voice coming from somewhere behind us.

Toni gave me a look, then backtracked and pushed aside some musty fabric to expose a doorway—actually just a rough opening broken through the concrete wall.

The chamber beyond wasn't very big, maybe about ten feet square. Jack was standing in the middle of the small room with the red-haired girl from dinner. He held one of her fists clenched tightly in his own hand, and they were yanking each other back and forth. They were struggling so hard, neither one of them noticed Toni or me.

"Come on," Jack was saying as he tried to pry open the girl's fingers. "Hand it over."

She glowered at him.

"What's the matter?" Jack continued, gritting his teeth. "Don't you understand English?" He gave the girl's arm a sharp tug. "How about French: *Ouvrez votre main!* No? Let's try Spanish: *Abre su mano!* How about German: *Mach dein Hand—ouch!*"

As quick as lightning the redheaded girl had jerked her fist toward her mouth and bitten Jack on the back of his hand. Jack let go, and she instantly pulled loose and darted toward the exit. She might have escaped, too—if Toni and I hadn't been blocking the way.

Seeing us, her big green eyes went even wider. She backpedaled into the room, stepping onto a mattress and smacking into the far corner. There she slid down into a sitting position, her eyes darting around wildly from Jack to Toni to me. She looked like a trapped animal.

"Jinxes!" the girl shouted. "Jinxes! Can't haves! I finded it! Squarelike and fairlike! Jinxes!" Her voice was shrill and insistent.

"What's going on, Jack?" Toni asked. "What does she have?"

"All of her grown-up teeth, surprisingly," Jack replied, rubbing his bitten hand. I could see a deep football-shaped bite mark over two of his knuckles. "*And* she has Ethan's Pez dispenser," he added accusingly.

"Jinxes!" the girl repeated from her corner. "Jinxes!" Whatever she held in her fist—both fists now—she was clutching it to her chest so tightly, you'd think her life depended on it.

"Are you sure?" I asked Jack.

"Sure, I'm sure," Jack said. "Look." Leaning forward, he crossed his eyes and poked his tongue out at the girl.

No one out of kindergarten would be insulted by such a move. But then again, I guess this girl had never *been* to kindergarten. Without hesitating she returned the babyish gesture.

Her tongue was bright purple.

"Aha!" Jack said triumphantly, pointing. "See!"

Realizing she'd been caught red-handed (or purpletongued), the girl quickly sucked the evidence back between her lips.

"I noticed her tongue was purple at dinner," Jack explained. "And when I followed her back here, I saw her playing with Ethan's Pez dispenser."

"Jinxes, jinxes, jinxes!" the girl growled through her clenched teeth, apparently trying to keep her tongue hidden.

I'd had enough of this. "Why does she keep saying 'jinxes'?" I asked.

"Maybe it's some futuristic swearword," Toni guessed. "You know, like when someone says 'curses'?"

"Oh yeah?" said Jack, considering this. He turned back to the girl angrily. "If that's the case, then 'jinxes' right back at you, Red."

"It's not a curse," came Whistler's voice behind me.

He had entered the room so quietly, I hadn't even heard him. "Jinx is her name."

"You sure have strange names here," said Toni as the skinny boy came up beside her. "Back in our time, people had names like Michael and Sarah and Dave."

"It's her nickname," Whistler clarified. "She got it because everyone around here thinks she's bad luck. That's why no one will go out hunting with her. She always seems to find trouble . . . or steal it." He crouched down in front of the mattress. "Give them back what you stole, Jinx."

"Not stoled," the girl stated firmly, jutting out her chin. Then, whether she was tired of hiding it or just aware that her game was up, she finally opened her fist, exposing Ethan's Pez dispenser.

"Jinx *finded* candy-neck man," Jinx went on. "Squarelike and fairlike. *Finded!*" She shouted this last part defiantly, waving the small plastic dispenser for emphasis. Captain America's blue-and-white head bobbled back and forth on its stem.

Jack crouched down beside Whistler. "Tell her she can *keep* the candy-neck man," he said in a low voice. "We just want to know where she found it."

Before Whistler could say anything, Jinx spoke up. "Tell Jinx yourself," she sniveled at Jack. "Jinx *speakses* English."

"Coulda fooled me," Toni muttered to me softly. But not softly enough.

Jinx's eyes flashed hotly in Toni's direction. "Not have to answer you *nothing*," she said. Her cheeks were flushed red with anger. Combined with her flamelike hair, it made her head look like a green-eyed comet.

"But—"

"No butses!" Jinx snapped, cutting Jack off. "You *giveded* Jinx nothing, Jinx *sayses* nothing." She held up the Pez dispenser. "Already haves what I wantses, besides," she added, her emerald eyes locking focus in Toni's direction. "Mostly."

I followed her gaze but didn't see anything—until my eyes fell on Toni's necklace. The tiny gold rope chain was just visible above the neck of her shirt, glinting in the candlelight like a strand of yellow sunshine.

Jinx's eyes were also glinting as she stared at the necklace. Her purple-stained tongue came out to lick her chapped lips. Greedily.

*She wants us to bribe her!* I realized with a shock.

Jack must have realized this, too. "Um . . . Toni?" he said, looking uncomfortable.

Toni looked in his direction. "Hmm?"

Jack cleared his throat and gestured at his neck.

Toni stared at him blankly. "What is it?" she asked, not getting his hint.

Jack sighed. He tapped his neck again, then rolled his eyes meaningfully in Jinx's direction.

"What?" Toni frowned. "Is something wrong with your throat?"

"No," Jack said under his breath. "It's just that, um, I think Jinx here is, uh, trying to tell us to, ah—"

"For crying out loud, Jack," I interrupted. "For someone

who can speak a zillion languages, you sure have problems spitting things out." I turned to Toni. "What the master communicator's trying to say, Toni, is that Little Orphan Annie here won't tell us where she found Ethan's Pez dispenser until we give her something else she wants. Like your necklace."

"Oh." Toni blinked, glancing down at her necklace. "I see." She frowned, biting her lip. Then her eyes swept around Jinx's decrepit little room. She made her decision.

Sighing, she reached behind her neck and unfastened the thin gold chain. Stepping forward, she held it out toward Jinx—gingerly, like someone offering a biscuit to a starving dog. "If I give you this, Jinx, do you promise to take us to where you found the candy-neck man?" she asked.

Lightning quick, Jinx's small arm snaked out and grabbed the piece of jewelry, like a bullfrog snagging a fly. She grinned widely.

"Jinx takeses."

Less than a half hour later we were Topside. As in aboveground. As in Ratsville. As in Sweeper Territory. As in Not-a-very-smart-place-to-be City. We were four dark silhouettes slipping through the night: Toni, Whistler, Jack, and myself.

Ten feet ahead of us Jinx was flitting through the ruins like some demented, redheaded pixie, just as proud as could be over her shiny new gold necklace. Supposedly she was leading all of us to the place where she "finded" Ethan's Pez dispenser. I couldn't see her—she was too far ahead—but I occasionally caught a glimpse of the light cast by her flashlight, a small golden disk crawling over the broken asphalt.

We each had a flashlight, which we'd gotten from the professor. They were his own design. They didn't run on batteries like regular flashlights but were powered by a hand-operated generator. You had to pump a spring-loaded grip in order for the bulb to light. The faster you pumped, the more light it generated. Unfortunately the more noise it made, too: just a faint whizzing sound, but still loud enough to draw unwanted attention. And not wanting anyone—or thing—to hear us, the five of us each pumped our lights just fast enough to make the faintest glow.

Even so, each of us older kids carried a crossbow, too. Just in case.

"Why does Jinx talk like that, Whistler?" I asked.

When he answered, his voice was surprisingly sharp. "It's a miracle that she talks at all. Considering."

"Considering what?" I asked.

We were both whispering. Partly because we needed to keep our ears open for the telltale sounds of Sweepers or rats. Partly because we didn't want Jinx to know we were talking about her.

Whistler pumped his flashlight a little faster. He dropped his voice until it was barely audible over the soft whirring.

"Our group found Jinx two years ago. Duck."

When it became obvious that I hadn't understood him, Whistler elbowed me painfully out of his way, then fired off an arrow into the murky gloom. I heard the low *bingggg!* of the bowstring snapping taut, answered a split second later by an ear-piercing squeal in the darkness to my left.

Up ahead, Toni gasped.

"What was that?" I asked nervously.

Whistler was already reaching into his quill for another arrow. "Don't worry," he answered. "It was a loner. Male. Only the females hunt in packs. Just keep moving." He turned around. "You okay, Jack?"

Behind us, Jack had frozen in his tracks and was pivoting back and forth, frantically pointing his crossbow in every direction. When he saw us looking, he stopped. "Sorry," he said, "I'm a spaz sometimes. I mean, hey. A loner. No big deal, right? Nothing to write home about." He made a feeble attempt at a grin.

Whistler smiled back at him, loading the second arrow into his crossbow with a loud *crick-ick-ick-click*. "That doesn't mean there won't be more of them," he remarked ominously.

Then he turned back to me, continuing his story as if nothing had happened. "When we found her, Jinx was living Topside all by herself in an abandoned basement. No one knows what happened to her parents. But from the look of the basement they hadn't been around for a long time. It was disgusting. And Jinx was like some kind of wild animal."

Whistler paused. For a minute we walked on in silence, listening to the buzz of the flashlights.

"Anyway," Whistler continued, "we brought her back here. At first we thought she would die. She was real skinny, and she barely ate, even though you knew she must be starving. For the first year she didn't say anything. Not a single word. It was like she was in shock or living in her own fantasy world. Then last year, out of the blue, she started talking. Speaking full sentences. It turns out she's full of useful information about surviving Topside, stuff she learned while she was on her own. She seems to know a lot about the Omegas, too. Of course, it's taking her a while to learn to say things the right way. But you can understand."

"Of course . . . ," I answered, but my mind felt numb.

I couldn't imagine what Jinx had been through. Heck, I was twice her age, and I'd barely made it through the last six hours. She had survived years completely on her own. So what if she couldn't speak perfect English.

Suddenly we heard her shouting up ahead. "Jinx finded right *there*. Fairlike and squarelike. Right there, Jinx finded!"

Whistler and I joined Jack and Toni, who had already gathered around the small patch of light where Jinx stood. She was jabbing her little finger in the darkness. "Right there! Jinx rememberses. Next to snatcheroo."

Jack shone his flashlight ahead of him, revealing nothing but a tall, crumbling brick wall and some exposed girders. "Great," he said. "Now if we can just find the snatcheroo."

"That's Jinx-speak for a trap," Whistler replied cautiously, "so nobody move. Jinx, where is the snatcheroo?"

Jinx smirked condescendingly. "Right affront of you. Only a baby couldn't sees it. Right there!"

"I'm not seeing anyth—*whoooa!*" Jack flailed his arms like a windmill.

He had nearly stepped into a massive pit in the ground, probably eight feet across.

"It's a Topsider trap," Whistler explained. "There was probably some kind of covering over it once for camouflage. They dig them deep so anything that falls in can't get out. Sometimes they line the bottom with spikes just to make sure."

Toni gasped. "You don't think Ethan . . ." She let the question die on her lips.

My hands had started shaking. *Please, no . . .*

Jack was already crouching at the lip of the hole, shining his flashlight down into its depths.

He turned to us somberly. "He looks pretty bad," he said, his voice weak.

"*Ethan!*" I yelled, dropping my crossbow and rushing over to Jack's side. "*Nooo!*" I shone my light into the dark well . . .

And found myself staring at a half-decayed rat corpse lying at the bottom of the fifteen-foot hole.

"Or maybe it's a she," Jack continued, unable to suppress his grin any longer. "It's kinda hard to tell from this distance."

"You . . . you *jerk!*" I yelled, tackling Jack to the ground. It took him completely by surprise. His flashlight flew out of his hand, spinning away into the darkness.

"You think that's *funny?*" I demanded, grabbing his shoulders and pounding them against the ground. "You think it's funny to joke about Ethan being hurt? Or even *dead?* When for all we know he *could* be?"

Jack's eyes were wide. "I—I'm sorry, Ash," he finally said. His voice was shaky. "I didn't mean to . . . I'm sorry."

I let go of him, then got to my feet. "Good," I said. My heart was still pounding in my rib cage. I sniffed once, wiping my nose with the back of my hand and brushing the hair out of my face. "Because it isn't funny."

Whistler came up beside me. He handed me my crossbow. Then he helped Jack get up off the ground.

"Hey. You guys. Look what I found," Toni called. She was standing a few yards away. We gathered around her.

Visible under the glow of her flashlight were a set of broad, booted footprints that seemed to vanish midstride.

"It's an Omega," Whistler said, "or maybe two. See where his tracks just disappear? That's where he got into his hover scooter. A scooter doesn't have wheels, but if you look closely, you can see how its engine kicked up some dust."

We followed the trail with our eyes. There it was—a slight disturbance, as if someone had rolled a large beach ball along the sand and dirt. The path led toward the distant hills.

"So you think he fell into the, uh, snatcheroo, and the Omegas got him?" Jack asked.

"Maybe," Whistler replied. "But maybe not. Look."

He pointed his flashlight at the strangest set of tracks

yet. There were three distinct kinds of prints: one that looked like it might be a foot, one that looked like it might be a paw, and one that looked like a big snake.

"*What* kind of mutant creature made *that?*" Toni gasped. "And *please* don't tell me *it* went in the stew," she added hastily.

"Easy," Whistler said, "a man with a wheelbarrow. It looks like he had a clubfoot, so that means he was a Topsider."

"So you think Ethan fell in the pit and the Topsiders got him?" Jack asked.

"It could have happened either way. A lot depends on whether he lost the candy-neck man falling into the pit or trying to climb out of the pit. The Topsiders could have got him, or the Omegas could have got him. Or the rats could have got him."

He paused, then continued quickly, "But I'm betting on the Omegas or the Topsiders. He must be very strong if he climbed out of that pit unaided."

"So which set of prints do we follow?" Jack asked. "If he could have gone in either direction."

"We don't really have a choice, do we?" Toni asked. "We have to split up and follow both of them."

"If we're going to do that, we should go back for provisions," Whistler said, "not to mention more crossbow bolts, and we shouldn't travel until morning—"

"There's no time for that," I put in, cutting him off. "We have to move, now."

"But—," Toni started to say.

"Toni," I interjected, "you go after the Omegas with Jack. Whistler and I will try to follow the Topsiders. There's no time to argue. Ethan's life may depend on it."

Moments later Whistler and I were headed alone over the desert. Jack and Toni were headed toward the hills, following the hovercraft's path—and taking Jinx with them since she refused to budge from Jack's side. If I wasn't mistaken, she was developing a little crush on him.

It was probably the first time in recorded history that someone had felt that way about Jack.

As quick as Whistler led the way, I wished we were going quicker. Ethan was in trouble. I knew it, somehow. And I was going to save him. No matter what it took.

# Chapter 10

# Ethan

"Move your feet, Silverblood!"

I was being led through an underground maze of tunnels where the damp air reeked of sulfur. After my escape attempt I was blindfolded and escorted out of the old hockey rink by four surly guards in long black robes carrying torches. Kind of a Grim Reaper quartet.

We marched along for at least an hour before they removed my blindfold. Then we descended a long, steep set of steps before arriving at a tall black iron gate.

The shortest of the four Reapers stepped forward and unlocked the gate. Another shoved me inside. They pulled the gate shut with a great *clank*, then turned away, leaving me there. All I could hear was the echo of their heavy footsteps fading away in the darkness.

I advanced inside the dank cell and soon discovered that I wasn't alone. In the dim light I could see at least twenty-five other prisoners. Most of them appeared to be in their twenties. Some were older, even middle-aged. A few were closer to my age.

They all looked surprisingly human. They all had

their own skin, hair, eyes, and noses and all their appendages—pluses in my book.

But they remained completely silent. No one breathed a word or uttered an audible sigh or grunt. Dread hung over them like a heavy fog that wasn't going to lift anytime soon.

"What are they going to do to us?" I asked no one in particular.

Silence.

"Why are we here?" I tried again.

No reply.

"Somebody answer me!" I demanded, my words bouncing around in the cavernous chamber.

Finally a scraggly kid stepped forward. He was probably my age. There were dark circles under his eyes. "It's the Fight," he said. "They say if you win, you win your freedom."

"And if I lose?" I asked.

"Then you don't," he replied.

The way he put it, I had no doubt what he meant. This was going to be a fight to the death.

I wondered if I had anything left worth fighting for. My friends might already be dead. And yet there still was hope. *"Another* silverblood"—that's what they'd said back at the market when they saw the cut on my arm. Did that mean that Jack, Toni, and Ashley had been caught, too? Could they be nearby, in another cell, and I didn't even know it?

I turned back to the young captive.

"Have you seen or heard about other kids like me—um, silverbloods—down here?" I asked him.

But before he could answer, the iron gate opened again. I turned around to see that the Grim Reapers had returned.

"You," the head Reaper said, pointing at me. "Come with us."

"Uh, can you come back later?" I said. "I was just starting to get acquainted with these folks."

*Bzzzzzzt!*

I suddenly found myself on the ground, writhing in pain. The head Reaper had zapped me with some kind of electric prod.

"Come with us," he insisted. "*Now.*"

"Gosh," I said, rising slowly to my feet. "Can't a guy make friends anymore?"

I gave a general wave of my hand to the other captives as the Reapers grabbed me. "Wish me luck," I told them.

I had a feeling I'd need it.

# _____ Chapter 11

# Toni

I had no idea where I was being led, but something told me it wasn't anywhere good.

For one thing, Jack Raynes was with me, always a sure sign that I'm not going to have a good time. For another, the individual doing the leading was a six-year-old pixie with a mean streak and a speech impediment.

And did I mention that the six-year-old was wearing *my* best gold necklace? I mean, I have to applaud her desire to accessorize. It's never too early to start. But if I were her stylist, I would give her two pieces of advice.

First of all, concentrate on the big problems. For one: You're wearing a burlap sack.

Second of all, try accessorizing with things that *aren't mine.*

The minute we got where we were going, I was taking that necklace back. It practically *made* my entire outfit. Not that I had much of an outfit remaining. *You* try crawling through fifty miles of rat tunnels while keeping your whites white and your brights bright. If clothing speaks a language, my twinset was saying, *Wash me.*

"Do you think this is Central Avenue?" Jack asked suddenly.

At one time Central Avenue had been a wide, four-lane street that cut straight through the Metier, right through the downtown area. "Maybe it was Central Avenue once," I replied. "But it's definitely not anymore."

"Me and my friends used to skateboard along the shoulder of Central on our way to the Metier Mall," Jack said. "Sometimes we'd even piggyback on the back of the local bus. That's where you grab onto the rear fender and let it pull you along."

"I know," I replied. "I used to watch you as we drove past."

"You can pick up some pretty good speed that way," Jack continued. "I suppose if my mom had ever found out about that, she would have flipped out. Even my stepdad, Thad—who's pretty cool about most things—was always warning me to keep off Central. They both thought it was too dangerous, but that didn't stop me."

I snorted. "I wonder what they would think about Central now that it's patrolled by laser-shooting robots, tainted with nuclear radiation, and teeming with killer rats?"

Jack laughed at that, then abruptly stopped.

"What?" I asked. "What is it?"

"I miss Mom and Thad," he said. From the way he said it, I could tell he meant it. "It's weird," he continued. "I saw them both less than two days ago. But that was back in the 1990s—and that's, like, a million years ago. In this time—here and now—Mom and Thad are both dead."

I thought about my father, whom I'd also left back in the past. "They aren't dead, Jack," I told him softly. "They just aren't here right now. That doesn't mean you

74

won't ever be with them again. We'll get back to the past. I know it."

We rounded a bend. And that was when we saw it.

For years there had been talk about alien sightings over the Metier reservoir. There were so many reports—mainly from truckers and schoolkids—that the police stopped responding to them. But they shouldn't have.

Because now the entire Metier reservoir was covered with a vast silver bubble that seemed to pulse and glow from some inner light. Huge portals ringed its base, about three stories off the ground.

As I looked at the structure a whole string of vocabulary words sprang into my mind. Words like *indestructible, indomitable, impregnable*. And, oh yeah, one other word: *yikes*.

It was the largest thing I'd ever seen. It was as advanced and intimidating as the rest of Metier was devastated and lifeless.

"Welcome to the Terror Dome," Jack said flatly.

Neither of us had expected to find anything quite like this. I was beginning to wish we had taken Whistler up on his offer to get additional equipment. "How does anyone get in?" I asked.

"Omegas rideses in on scootches," Jinx explained. "Up tops."

By "scootches," I took it she was referring to the Omegas' hover scooters. In fact, now that I looked closely, I could see the vehicles pouring into the top of the dome, like bees into a hive.

"They've got to have guards up there," I said.

"Or at the least Omegas getting on or off their scootches," Jack put in, "which is just as bad."

"Maybe we can get in through those holes in the side," I suggested. "They're kind of high up, but still. There could be some way—maybe rungs set into the side of the dome, or if we find a rope—"

"Not good idea," Jinx said flatly, cutting me off.

"Why not?" I asked, peeved. No way was some bratty little six-year-old going to tell me what to do.

"Not good idea," she repeated in that same dry tone.

"But why isn't it a good idea?" I demanded. "Just because the holes are high off the ground? Or maybe because *you* didn't think of it?"

Suddenly huge jets of raw blue flame roared out of the portals all around the dome. Even from where we stood, over a half mile away, we could feel the heat against our faces.

"*Not* good idea," Jinx said again, with the faintest trace of a smug smile. I have never been a big fan of kids under nine, and I was beginning to remember why.

"Exhaust ports," Jack commented. "They had the same thing in *Space Blasters II*."

Almost at the same moment a small, beetle-shaped pod rocketed out of the top of the dome. It shot straight into a whirling vortex of clouds—

Then disappeared in a brilliant flash of light.

It was the time machine!

They were sending more Omegas back into the past,

I was sure of it. *But why?* I wondered. *Haven't they already won?*

"Brace yourselfses," Jinx yelled, tossing herself to the ground and throwing her hands over her head.

I may be slow, but I'm not stupid. By this time I knew enough to listen to her advice. I grabbed on to the nearest thing—Jack, as it turned out—and held tight. In an instant the earth was rocked by another quake. It was just as if the ground had been replaced by a huge water bed and a very fat person was jumping at the other end.

It was over as quickly as it had begun. I disentangled myself from Jack—who was being pretty nice about the fact that I'd almost crushed him to death—and straightened out my blouse. "That always happenses," Jinx informed us, "when Omegas blastses off."

"Well, at least now we know how we *don't* get in," I said tartly. "Does anyone know how we *do* get in?"

Jack and I were silent for a minute, staring at the huge, imposing structure. Both of us were thinking the same thing: *There's no way.* Then, as I somehow knew it would, a small voice piped up from behind us.

"Jinx knowses way in," Jinx said. "But might not tellses you. Unless . . ."

I turned to see her pointing at my gold bracelet.

*I don't believe this!*

"She's a six-year-old extortionist," I told Jack.

Jack just shrugged. "They say you can't put a price on friendship. . . ."

I sighed. I knew he was right. Ethan could be somewhere under that creepy silver dome. If he was, we had to save his life.

Jinx was grinning greedily, never taking her eyes off the gold dangling on my wrist.

If I wanted to get in, I was going to have to pay.

# _____Chapter 12

## Ashley

*This won't be so bad,* I told myself. *Just pay the man at the door and walk right in. Pretend that nothing out of the ordinary is going on. Pretend that you fit in. Pretend he has a nose.*

If only it were that simple. But I knew it wouldn't be.

From our hiding place a couple hundred yards away, I watched the long line of freakish-looking Topsiders who were waiting for their chance to get into an enormous public hall. Actually "hall" is stretching it—it was little more than a giant burlap tent, looking like a circus that had seen better days. And thousands of worse ones.

I made a mental note: If we ever got back to the past, I was going to invest all my money in burlap.

The Topsiders waited impatiently, shuffling from foot to foot and occasionally breaking into fistfights. It looked like the admission line to hell.

A vendor with a rusty food cart worked the line, selling some kind of fried meat on a stick. Somehow I didn't think it was corn dogs.

At the head of the line a huge, muscle-bound man, stripped naked to the waist—and yes, without a nose—received payment from each of the patrons. In a world without mints to print up money, this meant an assortment of rat pelts, old car parts, broken appliances, and clothing that was out of date back in 1976.

"It's going to be okay, isn't it, Whistler?" I asked my guide. "We can just pretend to be Topsiders, pay the fare, and walk in, right? What's the worst that could happen if they catch us?"

"If they catch us?" Whistler thought for a second. "Well, they would pluck all the parts off us that they'd think they could sell. That means fingers, toes, noses, and eyes. Then the parts they *couldn't* sell—" He gestured toward the food cart.

"Okay!" I interrupted quickly. "Let's forget about that. Let's concentrate on just getting in without being noticed, all right?"

"Sure," he said. He looked at me thoughtfully. "We're going to need disguises. I might be able to pass as a Topsider, but you're much too pretty."

I blinked and looked down at my feet.

So there it was. A boy was finally calling me pretty, and there weren't any witnesses. I hoped he didn't see me blushing.

Apparently he didn't because when I finally got the nerve to look over at him, he was bent down, taking off his pack. "What are you doing?" I asked him.

"We need disguises," he replied, "so I am going to make some."

He pulled out a knife and cut some eyeholes in a burlap sack he carried in his pack. Then he put it over my head. It smelled like someone had gotten sick in it. And if I wore it much longer, someone *was* going to—me. I tried not to think about what Whistler had used it for.

In a few minutes he had made a similar mask for himself. We looked like guests of honor at the all-body potato sack race.

Then Whistler poured some water from his canteen onto the ground. He stirred his concoction with his hunting knife. After a moment he had some thick mud ready to use. We smeared it over our masks, on our necks, hands, arms, and legs. By the time we were done, we had caked mud everywhere—even on our eyelids. We were utterly repulsive, unhygienic, and undesirable.

In short: We made perfect Topsiders.

After an hour had passed, we were near the front of the line. "Don't say a word," Whistler told me. "Let me do all the talking. I know how to sound like a Topsider."

"What if he asks me a question?" I asked.

"Grunt," Whistler replied. "It's pretty effective since some of these Topsiders don't have their tongues or vocal cords anymore. He'll just think you don't have yours, either."

When we got to the gate, it looked like we'd have no problem getting in. Then without warning, the noseless guard stopped us. "You two are pretty young to be traveling by yourselves," he remarked. "Where are you from?"

"Nowhere," growled Whistler.

"How about you, little girl?" he asked me.

"*Grrrrrrrrrunt.*"

"What's wrong with her?" the guard asked Whistler.

"Nothing that *these* won't fix," he said, holding out his hand. He opened it, revealing three crumpled pink packets of Sweet'n Low. Just like the kind my dad put in his coffee.

*Great*, I thought. *Now we're in for it.*

But the guard reacted as if we'd just shown him a stack of gold coins. His eyes went wide. Looking from side to side to see if he was being watched, he snatched the packets out of Whistler's hands, holding them as if they were a rare treasure. Then he pulled the gate aside.

"Step through," he barked.

We stepped into the covered arena. It seemed like I had asked all the right questions. All except for the one it was now too late to ask: *Is this a smart idea?*

# _____ Chapter 13

# Jack

"Is this a smart idea?" I asked Toni as we struggled to balance on top of a crumbling rock wall. The ground looked like it was weaving back and forth several stories below us.

I tried to remember if I had a fear of heights. Nothing was coming to mind, but given all the new fears I'd acquired in the last day—including mutant rats, toxic radiation, and giant, well-armed floating eyeballs—I figured heights might be in there somewhere.

"It had *better* be a good idea," Toni said dryly. "I'm all out of jewelry."

Jinx, who had apparently never even *heard* of the fear of heights, was running back and forth along the foot-wide ledge, giggling delightedly. She seemed to think she was on some one-girl, high-altitude version of *Barney and Friends*.

Jinx hadn't yet told us her plan for getting into the Omega base. She'd just pointed at the wall we were now perched on top of and shrieked, "Upses!" until we did what she said.

I'd been expecting Jinx to show us a tunnel or a secret stairway . . . *something*. Some actual way to get into the aliens' compound—which I would have to stop calling aliens now that I'd learned the Omegas were a product of the United States government.

But so far, I saw no way in. So far, we had a wall. And Jinx looked delighted.

"Funses! Funses!" she was shrieking over and over. "Jumpses and runses! Funses! Funses! Jumpses and runses!"

"You know, I've read Mother Goose, and that's *not* in there," Toni told Jinx. "How do you expect us to get over *there* from *here?*"

"Jumpses and runses!" Jinx exclaimed. "Jumpses and runses!"

I squinted into the distance. The Omega compound was still several hundred yards away and looking like just as much of a fortress as ever. "Jinx," I explained, "the world's record for the longest jump is twenty-eight feet, ten inches. The jump from here to that dome is about ten thousand times farther. What are you talking about?"

"I don't think she has any *idea* how to get in there," Toni said sullenly. "I think she just pretended to in order to get my bracelet. Isn't that right, Jinxie?"

"Jinx does *so* know a way in!" Jinx insisted, stamping her foot on the wall, sending a shower of brick dust and mortar raining down below. "Jumpses crosslike and goses quicklike!"

"Jack, you're the one with the language thing," Toni said wearily. "You figure it out."

"Jinx, what do you mean by 'jump'?" I asked her, thinking I'd start with the simple things first.

"Look!" she yelled excitedly. "Here they comeses!"

I turned and nearly fell off the wall in shock.

A swarm of the floating eyeballs Whistler had called Sweepers had appeared in the predawn sky, racing toward us like a dark storm cloud. There had to have been at least fifty of them. Maybe more.

At first I thought we were done for. But as the Sweepers drew closer I realized that they weren't coming for us.

The Sweepers were changing formation as they flew.

Forming a single-file line, the humming metal spheres zoomed below us, one by one, on their way to the dome. Their flight path led them right past the wall. Not a single one seemed to notice us, even though we were only about ten feet above them.

*I guess they're only programmed to look down at the ground.*

"Jumpses *crosslike*," Jinx said carefully, as if she were trying to explain a difficult concept to a slow student.

"Jump across . . . one of the Sweepers?" I asked incredulously.

Jinx nodded excitedly. "Sweeper scootches!"

All I could do was stare at her. Fortunately Toni sprang into action. "You . . . little . . . *monster!*" she bellowed. "You expect us to ride in on one of those floating eyeballs? Are you *nuts?*"

I made a note to add "Toni when mad" to my list of new phobias.

Jinx looked as if she might cry. "Jinx makeses deal, Jinx showses way to get in . . . ," she sputtered, her lower lip quaking.

"Well, maybe I should have said so, but I was hoping

for a way in where I would still be *alive* when I got there!" Toni stormed.

"Not fairlike," Jinx whimpered. "Not fairlike. Sweeper scootcher perfectly good way in. . . ."

"*Perfectly good?*" Toni shot back. "It's the craziest thing I've ever heard!"

"I don't see as we have any other options," I said. "And besides, I believe her. I think she's actually ridden one of those puppies into the Omega base."

"So what if she did? I mean, *hello*, that girl weighs about as much as a dust bunny. Do you honestly think one of those things will hold my weight? Or yours?"

I looked down at the speeding line of Sweepers. They were still coming, one by one. But they wouldn't be forever.

There was only one way Toni was going to jump on one of the flying silver balls before they had all passed us by. There was only one way that she'd take the risk. And that was if she was so mad, so furious, that she didn't even think about the danger.

Fortunately I was just the man for the job.

"Well," I told her, "they look pretty steady to me. I think there's another reason why you don't want to try Jinx's plan."

"And what's that?" Toni asked, her eyes narrowing.

"You're afraid that she's right," I said. "You don't like the idea that a six-year-old can do something that you can't."

It was like I'd planted a depth charge. I could see Toni head toward DEFCON 1. Her eyes became little slits.

Her nostrils flared. If she were a dog, I bet her lips would have been pulled way back over her teeth.

Now was not the time to back off. Now was the time to push forward. So I did. "It's true," I continued, putting on my best "annoyingly reasonable" voice. "She wanted your necklace, and she got it. That ticked you off. Then she knew that your idea of going in through the exhaust portals was—and I'm just pointing this out—pretty *stupid*. We're talking totally *dumb*. And then she made you give her your bracelet—"

"What are you saying?" Toni demanded. "You think I don't want to try it because I'm *jealous* of that twerp?"

"Yeah," I replied, "that's pretty much it."

Toni boiled with rage. "Are you *mental?*" she cried.

"Am *I* mental?" I asked. "I don't know. *I'm* not the one who's in competition with a toddler."

"Okay, that does it," she spat. She turned on Jinx. "You. Brat girl. Show me how to jump on one of those things."

"Am *not* a brat," Jinx started to say, "am—"

"*Just show me how to jump,*" Toni cut in.

Jinx's eyes opened wide. It might have been the first time in her life anyone ever talked to her that way. Her mouth opened and closed without any sound coming out. Then she made the right move—toward self-preservation. "You standses like this," she said, demonstrating by the lip of the wall, "and jumpses just as soon as Sweeper's nearlike."

"Great. Out of my way," Toni snarled. A Sweeper was just zooming up as she stepped to the edge. Then without another word she leaped off.

I was sure she was going to eat it. The Sweeper was passing at least ten feet below us and nearly six feet out from the wall. But I guess those cheerleading moves really pay off because Toni soared through the air and landed square on top of the metal sphere.

The Sweeper bobbled in place, looking like it wasn't sure what had just happened to it. It turned from side to side, scanning the ground for its attacker. Then I guess it decided that it was imagining things because it started to move back toward the base.

"Well?" Toni shouted at me from on top of the steel ball as it carried her toward the dome. "Are you coming or what?"

A few minutes later we were all piggybacking toward the Omega camp, each on our own Sweeper. The surface of the Sweeper was warm and slippery, but by lying as flat as possible on top of it, I got a pretty good hold. Once you got used to it, it was almost kind of fun, like being in a giant pinball machine. Except instead of hitting the ball, you *were* the ball.

The dome was approaching at an enormous rate.

Wow. We weren't slowing down. In fact, we were speeding up. Suddenly I realized we were about to crash right into it.

"Uh, Jinx?" I hollered over my shoulder. "Is this supposed to happen?"

On the Sweeper behind me Jinx raised her eyebrows and shrugged.

Great. I was on an eyeball with a death wish.

"*Auuuuggggh!*" I screamed as we hurtled straight at the surface of the dome. Toni might have been screaming, too—I was yelling too loud to hear her.

Then there was a strange sensation, like we were passing through a very thin mist, and we were inside the dome. Just like that. I checked myself out. Mostly unkilled—that's pretty good in my book. We had passed right through the surface!

"The shell must be some kind of semipermeable metallic membrane," Toni called back to me from her Sweeper. "Or like the surface of a soap bubble—always shifting and forming new patterns."

"Very interesting, Professor Douglas," I answered, "but right now shouldn't we be worrying about how to get off these things?"

We were hurtling single file through a large round tube. It was barely wider than the Sweepers—the top of the tube was only inches from our backs. One Sweeper hiccup and we'd be smeared like jelly.

"The next time they slow down to take a bend," she replied, "let's jump."

"Isn't that risky?" I asked.

"I thought you like adventure," she answered.

"Sure," I told her, "but not adventure that hurts."

"Jinx, we're going to jump," Toni started to say, and then stopped.

When I looked behind me, Jinx was rapidly pounding her "scootches" on the top of its metal shell. In response the silver eyeball was actually slowing down. In a moment she had it down on the floor of the round shaft.

"Or," I told Toni, "we could just try that."

Five minutes later we were crawling on our bellies through the Sweeper tunnels, trying to find some sign, any sign, that would lead us to Ethan. We kept low to the ground. The tunnels, designed for Sweepers to travel quickly through, weren't really large enough to stand up in. Plus there was the continual danger that a high-speed Sweeper might just come along and mow us down.

Every ten yards or so we had to crawl over a metal grate, like an air vent. Mostly they looked down into darkness. But sometimes they gave a view of a chamber within the dome.

"I wonder if they have a bathroom in this place," I said idly as we edged across another grate. "I could sure use a shower."

"*There's* a news flash," Toni said, sliding up beside me. "I'm amazed that the Sweeper you rode didn't die of asphyxiation."

I was thinking of a good comeback when Toni gasped.

I looked down. We were passing over a large room filled with sophisticated-looking computer equipment. My heart stopped cold.

Directly below us an Omega in a long, silvery uniform had stepped up to one of the huge glowing monitors.

Now, I knew that we were in Omega Central, and it made sense that there'd be lots of Omegas here. Still, seeing one so close up chilled the blood in my veins.

As we watched, two other Omegas in black guard uniforms led a toothless woman with an eye patch into the control room. The hag had to have been a Topsider. She was probably younger than my mom, but she looked seventy thanks to years of exposure to the direct light of the sun. Forget Oil of Olay: This gal was ready for embalming fluid. The guards pushed her in front of Shiny Robe, who I realized was some kind of leader.

"What do we have here?" he barked at his two servants.

"A Topsider," the guards answered in unison.

"I see that," he seethed. "Why have you brought her to me?"

"Your Excellency," the woman stuttered, her voice sounding like gravel going down a chute, "I have heard that there is a reward for information about silverbloods."

At the word *silverblood* the leader straightened up, paying the woman serious attention for the first time. "You have, have you?" he inquired. "And do you have such information?"

"Oh yes, yes!" the crone cackled. "I have good information! Quality information! I can help you find a silverblood boy!"

I nudged Toni. "How lucky are we?"

"Shut up," she whispered through her teeth. "They're going to hear you."

Down below, the leader approached the old woman. "Then do not hesitate," he said. "By all means. Tell me."

"This morning a young boy—a fine specimen, with beautiful milk white skin, all intact . . ." The old woman was practically licking her lips. "He was brought for auction at the market. But he was cut trying to escape. That's how I saw." She paused for dramatic effect. "His blood was *silver*. Silver! I saw it with my own eye." She tapped her remaining eyeball.

"And is he at the marketplace now?" the leader demanded. "Who bought him?"

"When his owner realized what he had, he would not sell," the old woman replied. "He kept the boy for himself. He's going to enter him in the Fight!"

"That's where he is," the leader said, more of a question than a statement.

"Yes, Your Excellency. He is to be put in the Fight. Today." She looked around greedily at the wonders of the Omega dome, then back at the leader. "So . . . when do I get my reward?"

"Right now," the leader said. He clapped twice. "Eliminate her."

"*No!*" the old woman screamed, trying to tear away from the two Omega guards. She wrestled pitifully, but it was no use.

"And find out who was supposed to be monitoring sector Delta-4 and have them eliminated, too," the leader continued, not even seeming to notice the crone's struggles and desperate cries.

"Yes," the two Omegas answered in unison.

"Come on, let's get out of here," I whispered to the others.

Soon we were headed back the way we came. Crawling

was much easier once you were used to it. We came to a sort of crossroads where three Sweeper tunnels intersected. At the center of the intersection the tunnel floor consisted totally of wire grids.

We edged cautiously onto the metal mesh.

"Leftses next," Jinx whispered. "Then rightses. Then straightlike, then crosslike." She rubbed her nose and continued. "That's fastest way outses."

"Do you know where this fight thing is?" Toni asked Jinx.

Jinx shuddered. "Very bad place. Very bad men, very bad things."

Toni persisted. "But you know where it is."

Jinx nodded. "Jinx knowses. Jinx not likeses. But Jinx knowses."

I was starting to like the little twerp. She was a little like me: not afraid to tick people off. I reached over and tousled her flame red hair. "I don't see why they call you Jinx," I declared. "You've been nothing but *good* luck for us."

"It's probably because—," Toni started to say.

Then she suddenly fell through one of the grates in the floor and plummeted into the darkness below.

# ————Chapter 14

# Ashley

She made no sound as the rat was lowered into her mouth. There was just a kind of *plooop!* sound as the rodent— moments before an eight-pound ball of whirling claws and teeth—disappeared down the lady Topsider's gullet.

Then she swallowed, wiped her mouth with a napkin, and burped.

Around her the freakish crowd exploded into cheers and applause. Goods were furiously exchanged as those who had bet on the rat paid up to those who had bet on the lady. Well, *lady* is probably the wrong word. Given that she was easily four hundred pounds of Topsider, *human suckwad* is probably closer to it.

And the worst part was, she wasn't nearly the strangest thing I'd seen through the holes in my burlap mask.

It was as if Las Vegas had been taken over by *Ripley's Believe It or Not.* Everywhere you looked were the biggest freaks in existence. And everything could be wagered on, no matter whether it was a game of chess played with human bones, a race of giant mutant rats, or a contest to see which Topsiders could fit the most rocks up their nose. If they even *had* a nose.

I shuddered to think what they might be doing to Ethan.

It was difficult moving through the crowded tent. For an uncomfortable five minutes I was pressed right up against a huge holding cage of giant rats (or lunch, depending on how you looked at it) as the rabid creatures inside tried to claw and bite me through the bars.

Finally Whistler and I elbowed our way—or pushed, I guess, since some Topsiders didn't have elbows—to the center arena. If Ethan were anywhere, he would probably be here. I could sense it.

It was a circular pit about the size of a basketball court and deep enough to hold a two-story house. A circular rail ran along the boundary of the pit—whether to keep the throngs of spectators from falling in or to keep whatever was in the pit from getting out, I'm not sure.

All at once the lights above us flashed on and off. The crowd seemed to take this as their cue. A hush fell over the teeming mass of spectators. Wherever you looked, Topsiders were craning their necks, standing on tiptoe, pressing forward, all to get a better look at whatever was about to come into the pit.

I pressed closer, too, looking for clues.

There was nothing but darkness below.

# Chapter 15

# Toni

I was sliding down a steep, dark shaft, faster and faster—and I had no idea how long I would be falling. I pressed my palms hard against the metal surface, hoping it would slow me down. No such luck.

*I swear*, I thought, *the next time I see that little redhead, I'm going to kill her.*

How did I know that as soon as Jack called her a good luck charm, she'd prove him wrong? That's just an unwritten rule: If you happen to be having good luck, try not to mention it.

Particularly in front of someone named Jinx.

I thought I saw a speck of light down below me. Could it have been my imagination? No, there it was, and it was getting larger. Much larger. I suddenly realized that it was the entrance to a room, probably a skylight. I was coming in for a landing.

This was going to hurt.

They prepare you for a lot of things at cheerleading camp, where I spent last July and August with my then best friend, Lynette Barbini. Jumping splits, break and rolls, even how to make a human pyramid if the rest of your squad is, to put it delicately, a little on the plus side.

But they didn't teach anything about bursting through a pane of glass at speeds in excess of eighty miles per hour. I was going to have to improvise.

I tucked myself into as tight a ball as possible. Hopefully that would save me from being badly cut when I hit the skylight. But that left the question of the floor below.

I concentrated as hard as I could. I felt the hairs on the back of my neck start to rise as the power coursed up through my body. I didn't have much energy stored up, so I would have to make this count. My toes tingled with the effort, then my legs, my stomach, and my hands.

I couldn't help it; I peeked at the light below. I was too late. I was too close. I wasn't going to make it.

I balled my hands into fists, concentrating on the empty air ahead of me. It began to shimmer as electric current coursed into it. I pushed with all I was worth, my mind straining with the effort.

Then I hit the glass, like I'd just cannonballed off the highest high dive in the entire world. I was surrounded by a cloud of rainbow-colored shards that flew through the air, tinkling all around me.

I was uncut, which meant that my power shield was holding—at least it had so far. But would it cushion my fall? I was about to find out.

Faster than I could think, I rocketed against the floor. The room was a blur as I hit. One instant the world was in bright, screaming color, the next it was black. I didn't hear the *thud* so much as live it as my body hit the ground with sickening force.

If I had died and that pixie was why, I was going to haunt her clear through puberty.

Then slowly I felt sensation return. The shield had worked. But everything felt prickly, as if my entire body had fallen asleep or as if I were lying on broken glass.

*Duh*. I *was* lying on broken glass.

Feeling woozy, I peeled myself off the floor. Every part of me hurt. I was only grateful for one thing: that there was no mirror handy.

I was utterly drained. I had the full-body fatigue that hit me whenever I tried to make my power do tricks it hadn't learned yet.

But what I saw next made me jump straight up in the air.

The room I was in was empty except for six huge glass tubes, each about three feet wide, stretching from floor to ceiling. They were lit from within like aquariums and filled with yellow liquid. They looked a lot like the specimen jars Mr. Holland kept in the biology lab, filled with fetal pigs and pickled cow brains and dead frogs.

Two of the tubes in front of me held specimens. But they weren't pigs or frogs.

They were humans.

Humans I *knew*.

Todd Aldridge and Elena Vargas.

They were in their clothes, suspended in the weird yellow fluid, with their eyes closed. Todd's loose green T-shirt billowed around his stomach in an invisible current.

Elena's long, dark brown hair flowed around her head like the tentacles of a sea creature.

Have you ever been so horrified by something that you feel a need to simultaneously scream and puke and your mouth can't decide which it is you're going to do, so it winds up just hanging open? No? Well, let me tell you, it's a classy look for any girl. I tried it out as thoughts raced through my head:

*Are Todd and Elena dead in there? Can I rescue them? Does that liquid stain?*

Then an idea came to me. I remembered how the other kids had told me that Elena's powers were psychic. She had the ability to speak directly into someone's mind. Maybe it would work both ways. Maybe she could pick up on my thoughts and respond.

Still feeling exhausted, I pushed myself toward Elena's tube and placed my hands on the curved glass. It was an effort just to remain standing. Using my last ounce of strength, I sent my thoughts out to my long lost classmate.

*Elena*, I thought at her, *Elena, it's me, Toni Douglas. Elena, can you hear me? Are you alive? Elena?*

There was no response. My strength flickering, I tried again. *Come on, Elena*, I thought. *You have to be alive. Please, Elena, give me a sign.*

It was no use. Either she wasn't able to hear me—or she just wasn't Elena anymore. I stepped back, defeated.

Then Elena's eyes snapped open wide, startled.

She stared straight at me with a flash of recognition.

In the space of a few seconds Elena's eyes went

through a flood of emotions, rapidly running from shock to elation to relief . . . and then fear, urgency, and dread.

Her eyes darted to something over my shoulder, growing wide with fright. She opened her mouth as if in warning, but no sound came out.

I was too exhausted to turn around. I didn't even struggle as the viselike hand of an Omega seized my shoulder.

"Where are they?" the Omega demanded. "The ones you came here with. Where are they?"

"I don't know," I replied, my tongue feeling thick as a Beanie Baby in my mouth. All I wanted to do was sleep.

He pushed me onto my knees. "I'll ask you one more time. Where are your friends?"

"Why don't you pick on someone your own size," I suggested. "Or maybe someone much, much bigger?"

He raised his weapon—a short metallic baton—and pressed it to my neck. "Tell me where they are now, and I will give you a quick death. You will feel no pain. *Where are they?*"

Before I could answer, a flash of red came tumbling out of the air duct above us—a tiny meteor of flailing knees and elbows—careening directly into my Omega captor before landing on the floor. It was Jinx. The Omega reeled from the force of the blow but somehow managed to stay standing.

"What was—," he started to say, looking up into the yawning cavity of the ventilation shaft.

As if on cue, Jack came shooting out, feetfirst into the guard's head. It was lights out for the Omega man.

"Oh yeah," I told the unconscious Omega. "*There* they are."

# _____Chapter 16

# Ethan

"So long," I said cheerfully to my last set of Topsider guards as they handed me off to yet another squadron of Grim Reaper look-alikes. "Smell you later."

I was being treated like a human baton, passed from one guard squadron to another. I guess they had decided not to take any chances with me. Why, you'd almost think I was dangerous.

We turned down yet another winding corridor. "You guys ever get the feeling you're really just a bunch of mice?" I asked. "I mean, all these narrow passages. I bet you have tread wheels down here, too, don't you—"

*Bzzzzzzt!*

They answered me with another zap from their electric prods.

"I'll take that as a *no*," I said, rubbing my throbbing arm.

"Shut up, boy," the head Reaper ordered.

The corridor finally dead-ended at a bizarre mirrored wall that completely blocked off the tunnel. It made our reflections all thin and squiggly, like a fun-house mirror.

I turned around to my escorts, whose eyes glowed fiery red from under their roomy hoods.

*Is this it?* I wondered. *Is this the Fight?*

I sized them up. Looked for their weaknesses. I would take on the biggest one first: blow out his kneecap with a sharp, blunt kick. Then grabbing away his prod, I could handle the others. Maybe herd them back to the holding pen and free the prisoners.

They started to come at me—each holding out their electrifying weapons. I backed up. They kept coming. I was quickly running out of room.

Finally the head Reaper lunged at me with his prod. To avoid it, I had to jump back against the mirror wall. And not only did I hit it—I passed right through it! It was as if I had backed through a wall of liquid mercury.

I fell through to the other side. Into pitch blackness. I couldn't see my hand in front of my face. When I reached back to the wall, it was as solid as a rock.

Was that it? Had I just lost the Fight?

*Jeez. They could've at least explained the rules to me before I—*

My thoughts were broken as a bright, blinding spotlight shone down from overhead. Then a second light came on. And a third. There was an eruption of cheers above me.

I spun around, squinting in the mad glare to view my newly illuminated surroundings.

I was in a deep circular pit. The great-granddaddy of the pit I'd fallen into last night. It was a good forty yards across from one side to the other.

I looked up to see a large crowd of more scarred and gruesome humanoids twenty feet above. They leered down at me over a guardrail that lined the rim of the pit.

Then they started to chant: "Fight! Fight! Fight! Fight!"

I saw someone moving among them, fielding bets. It was the lipless Daggs. In his sun-fried mind I was his property. His pit bull.

*I don't think so, pal.*

I looked around for a means of escape. The smooth rock walls were too high and steep to climb. There were no exits or doors, just two large mirrored panels: the one I'd just passed through and another directly across from me.

As I watched, the surface of the far mirror began to ripple like the surface of a pond.

The chant grew louder and louder.

A moment later a large figure passed through the force-field wall. Upon his appearance the mutants burst into frenzied applause.

"Han-ni-bal!" they chanted now. "Han! Ni! Bal!"

*What the . . .*

The giant figure, apparently named Hannibal, stalked toward the center of the pit arena. It had to be the Incredible Hulk's evil twin. His arms and legs were like sequoia trees. His neck was nonexistent.

He weighed three hundred pounds, easy. And those three hundred pounds were all raging muscle.

My heart did a three-point gainer into my throat. I was *definitely* out of my weight category.

Hannibal circled me like a sumo wrestler gauging his opponent. He glared at me with enormous, bulging eyes. I'd bet the farm this freak spent most of his life in the dark.

The crowd was getting restless.

"What are we waiting for?" a voice shouted down at us. "I didn't come here to see a waltz!"

The other spectators added their own cries of protest.

A bell sounded from above.

Hannibal wasted no time. He charged me like a bull.

I dodged him at the last second and he flew to the ground, the impact sending up a huge cloud of dust.

A mixture of hoorays and boos broke out.

My vision wasn't all there yet. I was still adjusting to the bright lights, the new space, the massiveness of my opponent.

"Come on, Hannibal! He's just a kid!"

"Squash him like a bug!"

Hannibal got to his feet and came hurtling toward me again.

I got into my stance: shifting on my feet, fists clenched and tucked at my sides. When he got close enough, I threw a roundhouse kick to the side of his head.

But he caught my foot in midair. Twisted it sharply. I shrieked in pain.

He flipped me onto my back. Then went to do a belly flop on top of me. I rolled away just in time.

My adrenaline was on the rise again. My focus was coming back.

Picking himself up, Hannibal charged me again. I did a head-over-heels flip that landed me right behind him. He wheeled around and lunged. I grabbed his arm and kept him in his own momentum, hurling him against the wall.

New rules suddenly came into play. Reaching into his

boot, Hannibal withdrew a wicked-looking dagger. He cocked his arm and let it fly right for my head.

By now my heightened sight was locked in. Not only did I see the blade coming at my forehead, I could see the speckles of rust on it.

With reflexes that astonished even me, I reached out and snatched the knife by the handle. Maybe an inch— two at the most—from my head.

"Ahhhhhhhhs" floated down from the stands.

"Close," I said. "But no cigar, muscle head." Then I fired the dagger back, purposely missing him. The metal blade whizzed past his head, glinting off the stone wall behind him, sending up tiny sparks where it hit.

Enraged, Hannibal lunged at me, swinging his meaty fist at my head.

I blocked his punch, then—*poom! poom!*—did a cross jab to his face, a fly kick to his gut.

And for the first time I heard him groan.

I got back into position. Regained my balance. Then drove my heel to the back of his head, throwing a battery of knuckles to his solar plexus.

His legs were getting wobbly. This sequoia was going down.

I stepped back and readied myself yet again. Time for the clincher: I jumped straight up in the air, did a 360, and—*bam!*—delivered a hard hook kick to his temple. I waited for a moment and did the exact kick to the other side.

Hannibal just stood there in a daze. His bulging eyes

seemed to be getting smaller and smaller. He lunged at me a final time . . . but only fell forward.

"Timber," I whispered.

He landed face first, sending a rippling tremor throughout the pit.

I stepped away. The fight was over.

But the mutants didn't think so. They unleashed a wave of boos and hisses at me.

"Finish him off, Silverblood!" a voice cried.

"The loser must die!" another shouted.

I looked up at them, waving my arms for silence.

"I have beaten him in fair combat," I shouted. "I have won the right to take his life . . . or to spare it."

They booed me. So much for good sportsmanship.

Moments later the Grim Reaper quartet appeared out of nowhere. They dragged off the unconscious Hannibal, leaving me alone in the center of the pit.

"I won the fight!" I yelled. "Now let me go!"

The stands erupted with laughter.

"But the party's just getting started, Silverblood," someone replied. "That was just the warm-up!"

The force-field wall began to ripple.

I was about to meet my next opponent. Or should I say, next victim? I was hitting my stride and feeling cocky.

Until I saw what they had in store for me.

# _____ Chapter 17

# Jack

It didn't look good.

My eyes frantically scanned the control panels at the base of Elena and Todd's holding tanks, looking for the magic switch that would release them.

Even though I can read a bunch of languages, it doesn't help if nothing's labeled. The panels on the tubes were just a confusing jumble of unmarked, glowing buttons. I guess I could have just started pushing buttons at random, but who knew what the result would be? Somehow Elena and Todd were being kept alive in the liquid-filled tanks. What if I pushed the wrong button and the life-support system malfunctioned or switched off altogether? They could go belly-up, just like every goldfish I'd ever owned.

_Zzzzzap!_

I glanced over my shoulder.

Behind me, Jinx was crouching on the floor next to the unconscious Omega guard. Her sack dress now hung loosely around her small frame since we'd used her leather belt to tie the guard's hands behind his back. Even so, Jinx wasn't taking any chances. Whenever she saw—or _thought_ she saw—the guard stirring, she would zap him on the neck with his weird weapon until he was still again. This happened about every thirty seconds.

Toni was leaning against the wall a few yards away. I don't know what she'd had to do to smash through the glass ceiling without hurting herself. But whatever it was, it had her beat.

"Are you okay?" I asked her.

Toni nodded wearily. "I'll be fine. I just need a minute."

*Jack. Hey, Jack!*

I flinched as a girl's voice sounded loudly in my brain. I looked up to see Elena's deep brown eyes peering down at me through the tank's thick curved glass.

I'd forgotten she could do that.

*Don't worry about us,* Elena's mind voice continued. *You guys have to get out of here. Now.*

"But what about you and Todd?" I asked.

*There's no time to free us. Besides, Ethan and Ashley are in more serious danger. You have to find them. Before the Omegas do.*

"How are we supposed to do that?"

At first Elena didn't answer. Then her eyes rolled up into the back of her head until there were only whites showing. Her eyelids fluttered as she entered a kind of trance. After about ten seconds she looked back down at me.

*The corridor outside is clear—for now. If you go quickly, you can make it to the area where the Omegas keep their hover scooters. You'll need to take one in order to get to Ethan and Ashley in time.*

Obviously being in that tank had pickled Elena's brain.

"Assuming we don't run into any Omegas out there, just how are we supposed to find our way around? This place is immense. We don't know where anything is."

*But I do. I've been able to explore this whole dome in my astral form. I can lead you there. Show you the way. Look.*

She stared me straight in the eye. Fixed me in her intense gaze. Seemed almost to look *through* me . . .

Suddenly—*wham!*—it was as if a flashbulb had gone off in my brain. In a split second I *knew* the way as Elena's thoughts streamed directly into my mind's eye. It was like watching a high-speed movie on fast-forward. I was zooming through corridors in the Omega dome. Left and right, up and down. Hurtling around bends and through hatchways that hissed open mere inches in front of me until I ended up in a kind of docking bay where dozens of the Omegas' scooters were lined up in perfect, even rows.

I blinked, and I was looking at Elena once again.

*Got it?* she asked me.

"Got it," I replied. I felt a little dizzy.

*Good. Now go. There's no time to lose.*

I suppose Toni and Jinx had also "heard" our conversation because when I turned around, they were standing at my side, ready to move. Toni was looking much better.

We hurried toward the exit. Passing the unconscious Omega guard, Jinx gave him one last zap with his baton.

The hydraulic door opened with a hiss. Outside,

the long, dim corridor was empty, just as Elena had predicted.

What *else* could she tell about the future?

As we left the tank room I took one last look back at Elena and Todd. I hated leaving them here. Hated it.

Elena must have been reading my mind.

For as the doors hissed shut again, her voice echoed in my brain:

*We'll be okay, Jack. You'll be back for us. Soon. I've seen it. Just be brave.*

# Chapter 18

# Ethan

*Be brave, Ethan*, I told myself. *You gotta be brave.*

My new opponent wasn't nearly as massive as Hannibal, but there was something about him that seemed fiercer, more intimidating.

Maybe it was the iron mask.

He didn't circle me like Hannibal had done. Instead he just stood there and waited for the bell. He knew the drill.

The mutants were getting restless again. They stomped their feet and began calling for the second fight to begin. I looked up and saw Daggs, counting his winnings.

*Probably saving up for a new set of lips*, I thought.

The bell sounded again. Combat time. My opponent, looking bored, slowly made his way to the center of the pit. He wasn't going to waste any energy.

"Give me your best shot," he said, almost with a yawn. "Let's get this over with."

"You first," I replied.

"If you insist."

And in a split second he popped me square in the jaw with a jackknife fly kick. I reeled backward. He kept right on me, following with a double jab to my abdomen, my chest.

111

I dropped to the ground like a sack of bricks.

He waited for me to get up, standing in the attack position.

No sooner had I risen to my feet than—*wham!*—his right foot found the left side of my head. I fell again.

"C'mon!" he yelled, challenging me. "Fight me!"

I stayed down as long as I could. Buying time, buying energy.

I had to dig down deep. I had to adjust my strategy.

Instead of getting straight up like before, I propelled myself backward off the ground with my hands and torpedoed him in the gut with my feet. He buckled. I quickly took advantage—*clanging* his face inside the iron mask with a hard right elbow, then swiveling again to deliver my left. It was like ringing a bell.

The assault clearly startled him. Apparently Iron Mask didn't expect to have much competition. Fueled by outrage, he answered me with a furious assault of powerful blows to every vulnerable part of my body.

I recovered, recoiled, and answered in kind.

The fight went on like this for what seemed like an eternity. We exchanged punches and kicks like we were swapping trading cards outside Metier Junior High. Except neither one of us was a kid. Far from it. We were masters of the art of combat. We were two king cobras with plenty of venom.

Sweat streamed down my face and chest. It was pouring off Iron Mask, too.

You could tell the goons up top were loving it. They knew this fight was special. I had never heard so many "oohs" and "ahhs" in my life.

But as the battle raged on, it was beginning to take its toll on me. Even with my senses clicking in high gear, I could barely keep up now. It was all I could do to hold my own against him.

For the first time since my thirteenth birthday, I had truly met my match.

And then it happened.

Taking the offensive, Iron Mask faked a hook kick to my ribs only to strike a smashing blow to my head with a punch that had everything in it.

The searing pain was unbelievable. It was as if I could feel my brain bounce around inside my skull like a peanut in its shell.

Everything grew fuzzy and muted. The crowd noise above me turned into a muddled sound track. Iron Mask multiplied in front of my eyes. Suddenly there were five of him.

I lost my balance. Dropped to my knees. My end was near.

"Don't stop now!" someone shouted. "Finish him!"

"Deliver the death kick!"

As I felt warm blood oozing from my right ear I could see my opponent assuming the ultimate attack stance. Standing over me, he drew back his leg, preparing to serve for point, game, and match.

"Get up, Silverblood!" I heard Daggs roar. "You can still win! Get up!"

No sooner had Daggs said this than something totally unexpected happened.

Iron Mask stopped himself, lowering his leg. He

seemed to be looking at me differently now . . . at my face
. . . my bloody cheek. . . .

His deep blue-gray eyes locked on my own.

*"Ethan?"* he whispered.

It took a while for my name to register inside my throbbing head. I looked up at him.

*Iron Mask knows me? This guy who is about to finish me off?*

Then it dawned on me. This highly skilled warrior, with so many moves, so much power . . .

"D-Dad?" I finally heard myself say.

# Chapter 19

# Ashley

*"Dad?"* I whispered, repeating Ethan's words. Had I heard him correctly? Even with my heightened senses it was hard to hear over the noise of the crowd.

Suddenly everything became clear. We knew that Henley had gone out to negotiate with the Topsiders. And we knew that he had never been seen again—that he had probably been captured by them. It made sense that these barbarians would enter a man on a peace mission into gladiatorial combat. And it made sense on another level: Who else could even come close to Ethan in hand-to-hand combat? Ethan was a genetically engineered fighting machine.

And so was his father.

I turned to Whistler. "We have to get him out of there. There's no way he can win this fight."

"I think the Fight's over," Whistler replied. "He's on his knees."

"No, he's not beaten yet," I assured him. "If we could only throw him a rope or something . . ."

"If we interfere with the Fight," Whistler told me, "the crowd will kill us. Running into the pit would be like suicide. We have to think of some other way."

"What if we created a diversion?" I asked.

"Like what?" he inquired.

"I don't know." The problem was that the crowd was so wild, it was hard to think of anything that would attract attention. If we started a brawl, for instance, it would hardly be cause for disturbance—there were already two brawls going on at that very moment.

"Can we cut the power?" I asked Whistler. "Knock out those overhead lights?"

"I don't know where the power comes from," he replied, "and we don't have the time to go looking. What if I shot out one of the lights with my crossbow?"

"No," I told him, shaking my head, "they'd barely notice. They've got hundreds of lights up there." I clenched my fists, desperately looking around for something—anything—that would help. "We need something big. And loud. Something so big and loud that they'd have to pay attention even over the noise of this crowd."

Whistler smiled. "I think I have just the thing," he replied.

# Chapter 20

# Ethan

Iron Mask looked me in the eye and smiled—at least I *think* he smiled. His mask made it difficult to tell. Then his eyes darted to the guards.

"Keep fighting," he said, low, "or they'll get suspicious."

Knowing that the great fighter facing me was my long lost father—Henley—I found renewed strength within my battered body. I sprang forward into his chest, toppling him backward to the ground. The monsters above loved it. They wanted their sick Super Bowl to go into sudden death.

"Dad," I uttered through clenched teeth while we were face-to-face. "How long have you been here?"

"Three months," he said in a hushed tone before delivering a hollow jab to my jaw. I let my head fall back as if he'd really popped me one good.

"I came here," he continued, "to convince these Topsiders to fight with us against the Omegas."

I threw a roundhouse that stopped a half inch short of his temple. He collapsed expertly to the ground. No one seemed to know the difference.

"Omegas?" I asked. It was the first time I'd heard the term.

He tumbled toward me and took me down at the knees.

"The *other* bad guys," he explained. "The Topsiders think I'm an Omega spy. They're just keeping me alive for their little gladiator games."

As we continued to "fight" I continued to barrage him with all kinds of questions. Questions I'd been wanting to ask for a long, long time: What was I? What was he? What was going on here?

But he stopped me.

"Son," he said. "Not so fast. You'll learn everything, I promise. First let's figure out how we're going to get out of here."

"What about the walls? Can't we scale them?" I asked, shoving my father down hard against the ground and delivering a fake pile driver to his throat.

"No good," he replied, pretending to be in pain. "The Topsiders will just push us back down. We can't fight against all of them at once. Not without some kind of diversion."

"What about the guards?" I asked as he wrapped his legs around my head and gave me a yank that would have broken another man's neck. I rolled with it, piking my legs up and over my head and winding up back in a standing position. "If we fought them together, they wouldn't stand a chance."

"Ah, but you're forgetting," he replied, rolling swiftly out of the way as a flurry of kicks—mine—fell where his head would have been, "we'd still have to get out of here, and the force field we entered through only goes one way."

I was getting frustrated. I leaped high over the lightning-fast double sweep kick he delivered as he did a quick handspring and righted himself. "But what can we do, then? Just keep pretending to fight forever? Because Dad, sooner or later, I'm gonna have to eat."

He seemed to think about that for a second. Or at least I bet it would have looked like he was thinking if he weren't grimacing to simulate a response to my gut buster. "The only thing I can think of—," he started to say.

Then the auditorium was filled with a terrible, sharp, piercing shriek. *A whistle*, I realized after a moment. It was easily the loudest whistle I'd ever heard, like the one they blow at Fred's factory in *The Flintstones*. Above us, the Topsiders turned from the railing to look at something behind them.

We had our diversion.

# Chapter 21

# Ashley

Whistler's plan was simple: He would do what he did best, and when everyone was looking his way, I would uncage the penned-up rats.

Then, with luck on our side, the rats would run around and cause a scene.

As it turns out, luck was *really* on our side. Because no sooner had I unfastened the cage door than I realized we were going to get a lot more than we bargained for.

We were getting a rat stampede.

The huge rodents, wide-eyed in panic, exploded out of the hatchway, throwing the cage door back against me, which luckily acted as my shield.

The crowd of Topsiders didn't know what hit them. But they caught on fast. And the rats caught on, too: to legs, shoulders, and necks. There were at least a hundred of them—some as small as terriers, others as large as Doberman pinschers—a virtual tidal wave of fur, teeth, and claws.

Fangs gnashed. Tails lashed. Whiskers twitched. Topsiders went down as the frenzied rats barreled between their legs. Some leaped on Topsiders' shoulders.

Others scurried up the tent rigging. Whether they were looking for a way out or for their next meal, it wasn't clear. But I didn't care. Pushing out from behind the cage door, I squeezed past the screaming mob and met Whistler by the railing surrounding the pit.

"Whistler, give me your hand. I'm going over the rail."

"But if you fall into the pit, you'll be trapped!" he yelled over the noise.

"Then don't let me fall!" I snapped. "Come on, Ethan's life depends on us!"

Seconds later I was dangling from the lip of the pit, one hand holding tightly to Whistler's. I thought maybe the Topsiders or their guards would notice and try to interfere, but I needn't have worried: All around the pit, Topsiders were hanging over the rail to escape the rampaging rats. I just looked like one more person with the same idea.

Ethan and his father had stopped fighting and were just standing in the middle of the arena, looking around them in awe.

"Ethan!" I screamed at the top of my lungs. "Ethan, over here!"

He looked over, confused.

Why was he looking at me like, *That's got to be the ugliest Topsider of them all!* Didn't he recognize me?

That's when I realized: I was still wearing the burlap mask. I tore it off my head. "It's me! Ashley!"

Ethan's eyes flashed in recognition, and his face broke

out in a broad smile. He turned and said something to his father, something that I couldn't make out over all the ruckus.

Then the two of them ran over to the edge of the pit. Ethan's father bent down, interlacing his hands to form a stirrup. Ethan stepped up into his father's hands, balanced—and then he was flying up toward me as his father flung him into the air like a human missile.

It was a one-in-a-million shot. Ethan had to cover at least twenty feet and hit a target only about six inches on a side—my hand—while in midair. I don't know whether it was his superskills or incredible good luck, but to my amazement, he did it.

I felt all the details in slow motion:

The slap of his warm hand, sweaty from the fight, against my forearm.

Then his grip, as tight as a leather cinch, as it closed around my wrist.

Then the tendons of *his* wrist, like two steel cables, as I grabbed and held on with all my might.

Then the shock of realizing our combined weight was more than Whistler could support.

My eyes widened as we both fell, headlong, back into the pit.

# Chapter 22

# Ethan

Ashley's eyes widened as we fell back into the pit. I *knew* she couldn't hold me. But it had seemed like our only chance! Why had I been such a fool? Now she was down here with me.

Luckily so was my father.

And he was right there to catch us. Well, not catch so much as cushion our fall. All three of us ended up sprawled on the ground, but no one was seriously hurt.

"Hey, Ash," I said as we picked ourselves up. "Thanks for dropping by."

She just stared at me with a strange expression on her dirt-smeared face. For a second I had the weirdest feeling she was going to hug me or something. But then she grinned, pushing a strand of hair behind a mud-caked ear. "Yeah, well," she said. "I just *happened* to be in the neighborhood. . . ."

"Of course, you *could* have showered first," I said.

"Oh, this? Haven't you heard? It's the latest in postapocalyptic chic."

I laughed. "By the way, this is Henley," I told her. "My real dad. Dad, this is Ashley Rose."

He put his hand on Ashley's shoulder. "I knew your mother," he told her. "She was a good wom—"

My father's voice faded as across the arena, the mirrored wall rippled and an Omega in a silver uniform stepped through, shortly followed by at least twenty more Omegas in black.

We were trapped. I looked at the line of Omegas approaching us. A part deep inside me—the part that had been engineered as a human weapon—wanted revenge. Revenge for what had happened to my hometown. Revenge for taking away my parents and teachers and friends. Revenge for taking away my childhood.

I saw the pattern of attack in my mind. I would spring suddenly at the lead Omega, taking him out before he had a chance to react. I would disarm him as he hit the ground, springing back a step. As the rest of the Omegas turned to face me I would finish them one by one, with my father fighting from the other side. Our enemies would be caught in a deadly crossfire.

I crouched, preparing to charge, readying myself for the strike.

But before I could move, I felt hands around my shoulders, strong hands, hands that seemed to strike faster than I could think. I looked up.

"Don't," my father whispered.

"But it's our only chance!" I cried. "They'll capture us unless we fight now, and if we're captured—"

"How long do you think she would last in an all-out

battle?" he asked, gesturing discreetly at Ashley. "Do you value her life?"

"I hadn't thought of that," I replied sheepishly. "But if we don't fight, what can we do?"

"Nothing," he replied. "Nothing but wait to see what their next move will be."

The line of Omega guards stood firm. By now they all had their pulse rifles out and readied.

"Company, forward!" the Omega leader announced. "Set weapons to kill."

# _____Chapter 23

# Jack

It was coming up fast now. There was nothing I could do. Nothing.

Of course, this didn't bother Jinx one bit. Perched on the rear of the Omega scooter, she clapped her small hands. "Funses! Funses!" she squealed.

The third passenger was squealing a different tune.

"Jack!" Toni screamed. "We're coming in too fast! You're going to crash!"

"Oh, please," I said, trying to sound calm even though we had mere seconds before we became a permanent stain on the outside of the Topsider tent. "We're doing fine. Look, all I have to do to slow down is pull back on the throttle here—"

I demonstrated and recoiled in shock as a screaming laser shot out of the nose of the scooter. The white-hot beam sliced through the air, burning a giant hole in the tent ahead of us.

Okay. So it wasn't what I had intended. But it *was* a solution to our problem. Another second and we'd zoomed right through the flaming opening and into the tent's dark interior, like a tiger leaping through a hoop.

Inside, Topsiders scattered in all directions as we skimmed along mere inches above their heads.

"I thought you said you knew how to fly this thing!" Toni scolded me.

"What I said was, I thought I could figure out the controls," I retorted, turning around. "Which I can. Pretty much. In fact—"

"Jack!" Toni hollered. "Look out!"

I spun. We were headed straight into some kind of sunken arena, like a big pit, surrounded by what looked like a thousand crazed Topsiders—many of whom seemed to be wrestling with huge rats. Unless I did something and quick, we were going to crash right into the pit's curving wall!

"Hang on," I said, "this may be a little rough."

I threw the Omega buggy in reverse.

There was a terrible shrieking noise, as if the scooter were going to tear itself apart. The pit wall was coming up at tremendous speed. We hit the ground, skipping across it like a stone on the surface of a pond. We started spinning out. Finally we came to rest, safely and silently, at the center of the circle.

"See?" I nudged Toni. "Told ya I could fly it."

Toni didn't reply. She was staring at something dead ahead of us, her mouth hanging open.

I followed her gaze to see about two dozen Omega soldiers, all pointing strange weapons directly at us.

Or were they pointing at us? I turned around and saw Ethan standing a few yards behind us, along with Ashley and some big tall guy in what looked like a steel Jason mask.

The three of them started running toward us just as the Omega leader said: "Fire, anyway. Fire through them."

"What does that mean?" Toni demanded. "Jack, what does he mean by *fire through them?*"

I didn't have to answer, as it turns out, because the Omegas gave a nice visual aid. Raising their weapons, they pulled the triggers and sent two dozen lines of fiery death crackling toward us at the speed of light.

Just before the lasers hit, a large, muscular arm reached past me and pressed a button in the scooter's dashboard.

The vehicle shuddered as star bursts of multicolored light exploded in the air a mere foot in front of us. Somehow the Omegas' lasers were being deflected.

Iron Mask had taken a seat beside me. "What did you just do?" I asked him in awe.

"Activated the force shield," he replied.

"Finally!" Toni sighed. "I'm glad *somebody* knows something about this thing." She turned to Ashley and Ethan, who had crowded onto the scooter behind her and Jinx. "Hey, guys."

"Talk about perfect timing!" Ashley gushed.

"This is Henley," Ethan said, indicating Iron Mask, who nodded at us. He was just now flipping an entire series of little switches in the dashboard.

There was a humming noise as two flat metal panels in the front of the scooter slid open and the pointed noses of missiles peeked out.

I guess it *does* pay to read the instruction book.

"Run!" the Omega leader screamed, hauling butt toward the opposite side of the pit. His troops ran with him.

"Don't fire," Ashley said. "Our friend Whistler's still up in the stands. You might hurt him."

"Don't worry," Henley replied. "This is just a warning shot."

Henley punched the launch code in and pulled the trigger. There was a *whoosh!* as the twin missiles streaked across the pit. Then nothing.

"Guess it was a dud," I started to say.

Then the earth opened up in a huge chasm of fire and smoke. The force of the explosion propelled the scooter backward several yards.

"*That* was a warning shot?" Toni demanded.

"No," Henley replied. "It's our way out."

He was right—we'd blown a tunnel clear through the side of the pit.

"We'd better take off," Henley told me. "They'll be back soon, with reinforcements."

"Aye-aye, Captain," I replied. "I think we're ready for liftoff."

I flicked the ignition to *standby*. The scooter's twin hover engines hummed with energy. Then I kicked in the full power, yanking back on the steering lever. The scooter shot straight into the air, wobbled a little under the weight of us—I was amazed that a vehicle built for two could even hold six—and then leveled out. We were off.

*  *  *

"No offense," I told Henley once we were out of sight of the arena, "but you really ought to chill, dude."

Henley had finally removed the Topsiders' mask, and the face revealed underneath gave me the creeps. Not because it was scary or anything, but because he looked just like a forty-year-old version of Ethan. They had the same sharp nose, the same intelligent, blue-gray eyes. But now those eyes were clouded with worry, scanning the horizon.

"Chill?" he asked, seeming uncertain of the word.

"Yeah. We made it out," I informed him. "We're safe."

"You sound pretty sure for someone who's been relying on the advice of a six-year-old," Toni said.

"Come on," I told her, "did you see the way those guys ran? We taught them a lesson: Don't mess with friends of Jack Raynes."

"Is that the lesson?" Ashley demanded, her eyes narrowing. "That we're friends of yours now?"

"Guys, knock it off," Ethan cut in sharply. "We're right back where we started. We should learn from our mistakes. We're a team now, remember?" He turned to Henley. "Dad, why *do* you look so worried?"

Henley frowned. "Here's something you may or may not know. The skills you children have—they're nothing but prototypes. When the government genetically engineered the DNA that gave me and the other Alphas our powers, they were making a rough draft. Tinkering around. The finished version is what they put in the Omegas. Soldiers they thought they could control. Soldiers that didn't understand fear, or mercy, or compassion."

We were quiet for a moment, thinking about that. Then Ethan spoke up. "But how do you fight a soldier like that?" he asked.

"You don't," Henley said. "Not one-on-one, anyway. Your brain is your greatest gift. If you're going to beat the Omegas, you'll do it through the human powers of your mind—the ones you always had—not the powers of your body. Remember that."

There was such a sadness about the way he was talking, such a seriousness, that even I felt it. Ethan was looking more than a little worried. "No problem, Dad," he told Henley. "And if I don't remember, I'll have you around to remind me from now on. Won't I?"

Henley wouldn't look Ethan in the eye. He turned his head to look away from his son.

"Won't I?" Ethan repeated. The silence was uncomfortable. Ethan looked about ready to break into tears, and I couldn't really blame him.

"Omega fighters," Henley replied, "at seven o'clock. Coming in fast. Get ready."

The first two fighters were on us so quickly that we hardly even knew they were there before they started firing at us.

"Hang tight!" Henley yelled, and we all crouched low. The laser blasts burst harmlessly around us, but our scooter was tossed through the air like a kite in a windstorm.

"Our force shield won't stand much more direct fire,"

Henley said. With one hand he reached up and grabbed the steering lever, regaining control and pulling us into a steep climb.

After a minute we leveled off, and I braved a peek down. We were flying along at hundreds of miles per hour, several hundred feet from the ground.

Henley piloted us in a tight U-turn so that we were heading straight back at our attackers. "Are you crazy?" Ashley shouted.

When they saw us coming directly for them, the Omegas scattered. "Ruthless and utterly unafraid of pain," Henley told us, "but very easy to confuse. The slightest deviation from plan really throws them for a loop."

At the word *loop* he began banking sharply upward. It soon became clear that he wasn't going to stop—we were going to do a complete 360-degree turn like a stunt plane. "Okay," I hollered, holding on for my life, "this part isn't strictly necessary. This is showing off, isn't it?"

"Gets the job done," he replied.

I was beginning to like this guy.

Several of the Omegas tried to follow us into the loop and failed, their engines cutting out halfway around the circle. They plummeted to earth in a sea of silver and black parachutes. "Do we have some of those?" Ashley asked, trying to hold on to her lunch as we hung upside down at the top of the loop. "Parachutes, I mean?"

"I wouldn't count on it," Toni answered. "Not six of them, anyway."

"We've got company!" Ethan announced.

As we righted ourselves two more Omega scooters appeared about twenty yards behind us. There was one on the left and one on the right. And they were rapidly closing the distance.

"I can't get this thing to go any faster," Henley muttered under his breath. "It wasn't meant to hold this much weight."

Soon it was clear that we were going to become the filling in an Omega sandwich! I watched in sheer terror as the flat panels on both the Omega scooters opened up, revealing the same rocket launchers we had just used back in the pit. I had seen what one rocket could do. Now we were going to get hit from both sides. They were penning us in, and as soon as they were in line with our scooter it was going to be all over.

"How close are they?" Henley asked, all his concentration on the sky ahead.

"Fifteen yards," Ashley announced. "Ten . . . five . . . four . . . three . . . two . . . one . . ."

"Hang on!" Henley shouted.

Just as an Omega ship appeared on either side of us Henley reached under the control panel . . . and promptly cut the engine!

We dropped out of the sky like a sack of cement. Toni's hair stood straight on end. Ashley and Jinx were screaming. I held on to the ship for all I was worth. It was like the biggest free fall ride at the most dangerous amusement park on earth. Only Ethan and Henley seemed strangely unaffected.

Up above, the two scooter pilots had no time to react

as they fired their missiles at the space where our scooter had been just an instant before. Each deadly missile passed through empty air—before crashing into the other Omega's scooter!

Where there had once been two Omega hovercrafts, there was now an earthbound hardware store.

Henley turned our engine back on, and the little scooter lifted off again—mere feet from the rocky ground. We broke into cheers.

"We did it!" Toni yelled. "We beat them!"

"Not so fast," Henley said. "Three o'clock."

We looked to our right. A black horde of Omega scooters was coming in at an incredible speed.

"We can head back to the underground headquarters," I suggested. "We could hide there."

"That's the worst idea I ever heard," Toni shot back. "We'd be leading the Omegas right to them! They'd come with reinforcements and kill every man, woman, and child."

"So what are we going to do?" Ashley asked.

"We're going to cut our losses," Henley said, grim. "Now I want you to do exactly as I say."

We nodded.

"I'm going to steer us behind that bluff," Henley told us, pointing to a rocky outcropping. "When we get there, I'll tell you what to do."

I tried not to think what our pilot, the ultimate warrior, might consider "cutting our losses." I shuddered. Only one thought was on my mind: Was I prepared to do anything he said?

# Chapter 24

# Ethan

I was prepared to do anything he said. He was my father. He'd saved my life. He was the hero of the Resistance. Anything he commanded, I'd do.

"Get out," he told us, bringing the scooter to an almost complete stop.

Except that. "What?" I hollered.

"Ethan, there's no time for arguments," my father said. "Everyone, please, get off the scooter."

"But what about you?" Ashley asked.

"I'll be fine," he replied. "Just go."

"I'm not going," I told him firmly. "Whatever happens, I'm sticking with you."

"Ethan, this is no time for arguments."

"I'm not going to do it," I replied.

Toni, Ashley, and the little red-haired girl were already on the ground. Jack jumped off with a nimble leap.

"Son," Henley said, looking me deep in the eyes, "my only son, you are brave. And you are strong. But there is something you have yet to learn. Sometimes, no matter how badly you want something, you can't have it. Sometimes the price is too great. I would like nothing

135

more than to keep you by my side. But that can't happen."

He looked so sad. I wanted to make him feel better.

"But Dad, I *am* staying—"

"No, you're not. Ethan, you have a mission. You have things you have to do that nobody can do but you. This is bigger than my needs or your needs. Millions of people's lives depend on your doing the brave thing this afternoon. Jump, Ethan. Jump, and don't look back."

"Dad," I asked him, my voice catching in my throat, "don't you—I mean, *do* you—"

"More than you'll ever know, my son," he whispered. "Now go."

I hopped off the scooter.

He tore into the open air.

Minutes later, as we hid in the shadow of the rocky cliff, the Omegas passed overhead. There were dozens of them. Fortunately they didn't see us.

Unfortunately they went straight after Henley.

"He'll be fine," Jack said unconvincingly. "He's a warrior, after all, and a—"

"Jack," I told him, "I know you're trying to do the nice thing, but please . . . I need a moment to myself."

"Fine," he said quickly.

I knew what was going to happen next. I braced myself.

When the explosion came, I didn't have to hear it. I felt it deep in my soul.

*Dad, there was so much I had to tell you. So much I wanted to ask you. And now I'll never have the chance.*

I straightened up. Toni and Ashley were staring off at

136

the distant fireball in shock. "Is he—," Toni said, without meaning to.

"Yes," I said. "He is."

Ashley started to cry softly.

"Don't cry," I told her. "He would have wanted us to be strong."

I felt a tug on my arm. I looked down to see that the small redheaded girl had taken hold of my hand. I still hadn't learned her name.

"Home," she said, looking up at me with large round eyes the color of green glass. She gave my arm another tug, pointing off into the distance with her free hand. "Go back home now. Jinx takeses. Home."

*We will go home*, I told myself. It was more than a hope. It was a promise.

*Somehow we'll figure out a way to get back to the past. And figure out a way to stop the Omegas. Once and for all.*

I turned to my friends. My team. They were all looking at me. Expectantly.

"Let's get a move on," I said. "We have a long way to go."

## About the Author

Chris Archer grew up in New Jersey, where he spent most of his childhood wishing he had special powers.

He now divides his time between New York City and Los Angeles, California. When Chris is not writing books and screenplays, he enjoys going to scary movies, playing piano (badly), and reading suspense novels.

He has never been to Wisconsin.

Don't miss

# mindwarp™

## Face the Fear

Coming in mid-September
From MINSTREL Paperbacks